SECOND TIME AROUND

ACCIDENTAL VAMPIRE PI
BOOK TWO

AVERY DANIELS

Blazing Sword
Publishing Ltd.

Avery Daniels/Blazing Sword Publishing, Ltd.

Colorado Springs, CO 80907

www.blazingswordpub.com

Publisher's Note: This is a work of fiction. Names, characters, places, and incidents are products of the author's imagination or are used fictitiously. Locals and public names are sometimes used for atmospheric purposes. Any resemblance to actual people, living or dead, is entirely coincidental.

Book Interior Layout & Design by Vellum

© Cover Art, Layout, and Design by Molly Burton

SECOND TIME AROUND/ Avery Daniels. -- 1st ed.

ISBN ebook: 978-1-7355663-7-5 Print: 978-1-7355663-6-8

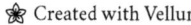 Created with Vellum

OTHER BOOKS BY THE AUTHOR

As Avery Daniels:

Resort to Murder Cozy Mystery series

1- Iced

2- Nailed

3- Spiked

4- Arrowed

5- Stoned (coming soon)

Accidental Vampire PI

1- First Bite

2- Second Time Around

As C.G. Abbot:

Elizabeth Grant Thrillers

1- The Society

2- The Legacy (coming soon)

"When the people have nothing more to eat, they will eat the rich."

Jean Jacques Rousseau: philosopher, writer, and influencer of the enlightenment, the French Revolution, and the development of modern political thought.

CHAPTER ONE

I, Misty Indigo Summers, was walking the last known location of a rogue vampire who attacked me and made me a member of the pointy-toothed club. The rogue vampire scares me more than anything else ever had, but here I was, walking the back streets of small town Majestic, hoping for a clue about the vampire behind several bite-and-run attacks in town.

A sickle moon was rising in the sky like a glowing fang. The Milky Way was conspicuous, stretched out above me like a gauzy and glittery fabric draped to decorate the night sky. The autumn leaves were falling, and the trees were more skeletal. A cool breeze played with my hair, tossing it about. The nights were growing longer, so it was only sevenish and I was roaming the several block area where the vampire attacks seemed concentrated. That was before Rowen and I crossed the rogue's path a few weeks ago and he disappeared.

My hands were sweaty and my mouth was dry from fear. I'd leave the fanged menace alone if it were up to me, but the local Meta community wanted him captured for breaking the rules. It was against the Meta-Mundane Council laws to turn a human without the proper permissions. I was just one of several he brazenly assaulted and left without taking responsibility for the life he had ruined. They thought I was a full-fledged investigator, so I was commanded to find him and bring him in if possible.

The good news was I felt nothing menacing, no sense of an apex predator right behind me like in a horror movie. I was scared spitless last time, but I thought maybe some inspiration would strike to point where the reprobate relocated in town before another poor person got attacked.

It was just five weeks ago that he attacked me as I walked home from the worst blind date of my life, which is saying quite a lot since I'd been on some terrible dates. Five weeks and my life had changed so much.

Sunshine saps my energy now. Thank heavens I live in a soggy part of Oregon; the lakeside community of Majestic. Its many rainy, drizzling days are a blessing. Yes, I am grateful for the dreary weather when I look on the positive side. The economy focuses on tourism and the tourist business focuses on our lake and its sports, so most locals curse the weather.

I can also now smell blood like a hound dog, but nothing else, sadly. Sleep is a distant memory already as I now experience a trancelike rest rather than blissful dreaming. I never thought I would miss dreaming, but I do.

The best part of this new gig was hearing my cat, Winston's, every comment which, at times was a blessing and other times maddening. I now knew how snarky my tuxedo cat really could be.

Becoming a vampire also introduced me to the "meta" citizens existing among us. I had met other vampires, witches, animal shifters, a dragon, a selkie, a gorgon, and a fae. The downside to the "meta" world was the prejudice. There was an Inter-Meta-Species Non-Proliferation Law forbidding, for instance, a newly turned vampire and a handsome witch, to even be friends, much less date. How absurd is that? I'm not admitting to anything, but Rowen is a great guy, even if he is a witch. Plus. the suave and stylish man taught dance. *Pinch me.*

An older green sedan turned onto the street and drove past me, stopped, then backed up. My instincts screamed to run, and I became hyper aware, like I would have to fight for my "undead" life. Some big-bad-vampire I make, right? A darkened window whirred down to reveal a thirty-something woman with shoulder length light blue hair.

"Miss, did your car break down? Can I help you?" The woman asked before she leaned over and into a streetlight's beam that made her hair appear electric.

I hadn't planned on questions since it was mostly businesses in the area and they closed around five or six. But I was happy it was a pleasant and thoughtful person to check on me. Particularly since my back prickled like I was being watched. A dog barked a street over, adding to my sense of unease.

I scrambled to come up with something to say other than vampire hunting.

"I'm trying to locate somebody I ran into a couple of weeks ago. He… umm… helped me out over on Pine, near the junkyard, and I want to thank him. I didn't get his name at the time. I got the impression maybe he was a night watchman or something because it was close to midnight." I held my breath, hoping it was be-lievable and she would give me some tidbit to follow. The dog stopped barking with a whine.

"Hmmm, could've been Jack. The plumbing supply warehouse on Pine had a watchman because of some break-ins looking for copper to steal. It was just about two weeks ago that he quit."

"Do you happen to know his last name or where he might've moved to?" I crossed my fingers, literally.

"Let me think, umm, Anderson, his name is Jack Anderson. I know that's a common name around here. I didn't really know him. I just chatted with the manager at the plumbing supply sometimes and he mentioned one morning there was a note from Jack that he had to quit. I doubt the manager knows much more."

"Thank you. I'll try to call over there in the morning. Thanks for your help." My shoulder blades still itched as if somebody was glaring at my backside.

"Do you want a lift to your car?" Her natural brown eyebrows scrunched together as a breeze scurried dried leaves along the street like bones rattling in some eerie wind chime and an owl hooted.

"I'll be fine. I'm parked close. Thanks Ms…?"

"Oh, I'm Charlotte. I run the self-storage lot over there and forgot my bullet journal. I had to come and get it since it contains my life." She gave a nervous chuckle.

"Thanks again Charlotte, and nice meeting you." I waved and trotted across the street toward my car a block over.

Jack Anderson was a start, even if it was one of the most nondescript and common names in all of Oregon. And probably not his real name. I'd take anything at this point since I had to show to the Meta-Mundane Council I was working to find him.

The deal I made with the vampire representative on the Council was Rowen could assist in the search for Vampire Jack and in exchange for help with my other investigations.

I drove home to my basement apartment with my own sunken entrance tucked under the stairs to the house above. I love my cozy one bedroom that I rent from a friendly lady that I used to babysit her children. I've known her most of my life. Mrs. Maksimowicz is my widowed landlady who owns the two-story home above me. The arrangement works perfectly for my new vampire status.

As soon as I walked in the door, my wonderful Winston greeted me. His short-haired black body with patches of white on his paws, chest, and down his face gave him a polished red-carpet aura.

You're late tonight. I was getting faint from the lack of food. You know how sensitive my system is. He plopped down on the floor and turned pleading eyes to me. I wouldn't have been surprised if he held a paw to his head to make his point. Since becoming a vampire, I've been able to hear him. That was a shock at first.

I got canned food for him, not his usual kibble. After my attack and subsequent vampire status, I default to spoiling Winston. He was dealing with my changes stoically, since I was becoming more of a predator to his senses.

"Oh, my poor little boy. I could call Mrs. M and have her feed you when I'm running late."

No, no! Don't bother her. I'll just patiently wait for you. I don't want to inconvenience that kind lady.

"You just don't want her to kiss and hug you like she does her Chihuahua, Maximus." I smirked.

Have you seen how tiny and skinny that dog is? She must not feed it because that dog's growth is stunted.

No matter how much I told him that was just the breed of dog he was, Winston believed Mrs. M wasn't feeding little Maximus, thus she wouldn't feed him any better.

I sat his dish full of rabbit pâté down on the floor and for the next minute he sounded like he was saying nom-nom-nom, or yum-yum-yum around mouthfuls of food. After nearly inhaling his food, he licked his paws and cleaned his face with a regal air.

"You shouldn't talk with your mouth full, you know." I said.

I wasn't talking, just expressing appreciation for the

meal. He let out a huff. It's amazing when you can hear your adorable pet and find out they have such attitudes.

We curled up on my tan couch, arranged the bright yellow and orange crocheted accent pillows provided by Mrs. M, and watched an episode of Beauty and the Beast on streaming. I could relate to the "beast" who is considered a monster and lives subterranean, but who does good. Even though it wasn't real, it inspired me that my vampire status wouldn't change me into an evil beast.

Like Vincent on the show, I could use my new abilities for good. I'm pretty sure Winston actually watched the show because he'd occasionally critique the plot with an *Is that really possible? Who wants to live underground, no fresh air or squirrels.* I kept from laughing at most of his commentary. If I laughed, he got offended. He was a sensitive cat.

I checked my watch. Time for my weekly call with Concetta, my vampire mentor, to educate me in the ways of this new vampire world I was tossed into. This time we were doing a video chat since she was *busy.* I suspected she was dating somebody.

I answered on the first video ring. I saw Concetta with her long black hair like Morticia from the Addams Family, only she typically had a dark blue streak on one side, but it was now a bright purple. She appeared to be in her fifties, but I knew she was much older. I had no clue how old, though. She still dressed like she was a hippie, with the tie-dyed top she wore draped off one shoulder at the moment. I believe she particularly enjoyed that era.

I opened our discussion with, "Why are vampires like false teeth?... They both come out at night!"

She didn't laugh but answered, "A vampire, like a lady, never reveals his true age." *Could she have thought I was joking about her age? I would never!*

Then she got down to the business of our video call.

"Okay dear, we left off last week with your asking about ever getting to eat food or drink again. I know how hard that must be at the moment." Winston pawed the phone in my hand and I let him sit on my lap and watch.

"When I was first turned, I loved the food at this place in Paris and cried that I couldn't enjoy it for a while. I don't remember how long it took, but at some point you tolerate sustenance again. I asked the younger among us… like those respectable young vampires Leif introduced you to a few weeks back. Justin, David, and Kyle had all been turned within the last seventy years, so they remember that phase more clearly." She looked at me expectantly, as if I should say something about the vampires Leif, the vampire leader in town, had abruptly introduced me to in the most awkward and least subtle move.

"Kyle turned just twenty years ago and thought it was about a year before he could take food again. David was only forty-three years ago, and he said it took him around six months, but some food still doesn't agree with him." Another pause, waiting for me to say something about Justin, David, or Kyle.

All three vampires were far better than every date I'd ever had in my life. But, I had already met Rowen and couldn't get him out of my blood. Even if he was a witch and forbidden. Besides, he likely only saw me as a quirky vampire friend. I didn't dare share any of that with anybody, even friendly Concetta. I was crushing on Rowen and the polite vampires didn't have a chance at the moment.

After a few awkward seconds, she continued, "I called an old flame who's a research scientist. He covertly conducts tests to figure out how vampirism changes the body. As far as he can tell, it looks like one's existing DNA will determine how fast the body changes to the new DNA structure, which also impacts how soon you adapt and can eat or drink again or if certain foods won't ever be tolerated. He's still trying to figure it all out. But one thing is certain, even after hundreds of years, we must have blood for nourishment or we go into a prolonged coma. But you'll get to taste food again, eventually."

I smiled. That was a relief because I had lost all sense of taste and I couldn't keep any regular food down. I missed Italian and Mexican food so badly. Although, the last few days I was craving Panang Curry Chicken fiercely. The cravings for my favorite cuisine were torture.

Is that what cravings during pregnancy were like? I'd never have to worry about that now. Or would I? It seemed to follow that the whole biting thing was how they created new vampires, so procreation must not be possible.

I didn't feel comfortable asking Concetta about that because she might think I had somebody in mind or had reason to worry. I didn't need her getting suspicious or pushing young vampires at me like Leif had done.

"Does that mean my smell will return too?" It was worth asking and the first thing that came to my mind other than pregnancy.

"Mine did, and since smell is so connected to taste, I'd imagine so." She said.

"I want to share with you the history of Majestic's vampire community."

"Please don't tell me it was founded by vampires! No, the witches?"

"No, a mundane founded the town, but Leif was the first Meta to find the area and realize the climate made it a good place for vampires to lie low and live peacefully."

"Leif? Is that why he's the head honcho of vamps in town?"

"That, and he has been a key part of keeping the meta-mundane coexistence without incident."

"Sure, sure. But could he learn some interpersonal skills past his raiding Viking approach?"

She chuckled, "He is rough around the edges, to be sure. But he also realized that too many vampires in town would draw attention."

"How's that possible when you are mostly night creatures?"

"And we rarely socialize with mundanes. Don't you think numerous anti-social misfits that only associate with other night dwelling anti-social folks would draw attention? He managed to keep it a well kept secret for many decades and then got a local council established to regulate how many metas of varying types lived here to keep our presence quiet and maintain the coexistence without problems. Too many vamps in such a tiny wilderness locale made sourcing blood from the nearest blood bank harder, as well."

That explained how I never suspected a thing, and why Leif was such a force in town.

After my video mentoring session with Concetta, I spent a couple of hours studying for my online class to become a licensed Private Investigator. The morning after a vampire attacked me, my boss took a sabbatical from his business to follow his wife and try to save their marriage. I couldn't afford to look for another job, which aren't plentiful in this lake-oriented tourist town.

I began doing what I could to clear the cases we had. I even solved a murder. Since my boss, Jared Hunter, is the actual licensed investigator, I've been hiding the fact that I've been doing the work and act as if Mr. Hunter simply isn't available when the police or clients ask to speak to him. I'm pursuing getting my license.

When you become a vampire, your natural proclivities and drives are heightened. My natural inclinations have always been to help people and I've found a purpose in investigating. I was always an average student, so I really had to apply myself to the investigator's licensing studies.

I was currently in a surveillance techniques course covering what legally can or can't be done. When I glanced at the time, it was after one in the morning. Yes, night time is better for vampires. We have far more energy and strength in the nocturnal hours than during the daylight, but I was determined to not completely upend my life because of the attack.

I kept a somewhat normal daytime schedule with bright days harder to power through than the overcast. I still wore glasses, only with no prescription, just plain glass, since I no longer needed them. It helped me feel my old self and I believe people took me a bit more seriously when I wore them.

I turned out the dim lights and retreated to bed with Winston curled up in the crook of my arm. *Good night mom, love ya.* "I love you, my little buddy." *He knew how to melt my heart.*

I had a feeling creep up on me that the day ahead would be monumental. I lay there, eyes open in a zoned out, trance-like state until my alarm beeped to start another day.

CHAPTER TWO

The morning dawned cool and overcast. *Ah, blessed dreary weather!* My basement apartment provided a rather dark dwelling, which is perfect for my situation. Besides, vampires need a connection to earth, so being mostly underground except for a few small windows near the ceiling was strangely comforting. I recited my positive affirmations for the day. I had adopted these after the attack to help me through the major life change being a vampire brought:

I take extra good care of myself and Winston.

I stay present-focused and take this one day at a time.

I choose to be optimistic. I get through this life change with ease and grace.

I focus on what I can control and release the rest.

I am stronger than I know.

I'd never been much of a morning person and since becoming a vampire that was compounded, but I was thankful for my job and getting to help people. Everybody makes sacrifices in life, daytime living was mine. Other vampires in Majestic found night oriented work or worked from home, but I finally found a job I liked at the only private investigator in town and it required daytime inquiries.

I went through my closet and chose a rust-colored pants-suit set I'd found at the local *gently used* boutique. It was my nod to autumn, plus I liked the color. I tried to dress for success, so I went for a more formal work uniform and I could tell a difference in how people regarded me.

My morning routine was streamlined without worrying about making lunch or setting out anything to thaw for dinner. *What I wouldn't give to devour a donut, though.* I'd been such an ardent fan of food before being bitten. I wasn't much of a cook, but all that inconvenience faded when you couldn't have food at all, even temporarily. I poured some kibble for Winston, but he didn't leave the bed. I'd never known any other cat that wasn't a morning creature. I must've rubbed off on the little guy.

The last thing I did as I left was to turn on the grow lamp hanging above my suspended plants, a Boston Fern and a Spider plant. They were part of the connection with the earth and nature that was necessary for vampire mental health and it gave me a little energy boost. I never would have imagined mental health was an issue with the "undead."

My rental didn't include a garage space, so I parked on the street. I'm incredibly thankful for my charcoal-gray two-door car with wide teal racing stripes, hand-me-down that it was. I really needed to name it, but all I came up with was Matilda. That didn't seem to fit. The gray seemed more mature, but the stripe was more youthful and the contradiction had me stymied for an apropos name.

I strolled out, luxuriating in the cool crisp air that provided a touch more energy. The coolness embraced me, wrapped me in its arms, and left my skin tingling. It was that in-between season where it was getting a little colder, but not actually winter yet either. I was now more aware of the seasons and weather than ever before. The overcast was gentle on my eyes, whereas bright sunshine hurt, and I felt a smidgen more alive and vibrant.

I went to my monthly therapist session. I'd been seeing Dr. Mercy Cresswell for a year before the attack. Her office was an oasis with a fountain providing soothing splashing water and a multitude of potted plants that comforted me. We primarily dealt with the baggage from my parents' complete lack of interest in me all my life that the Dr. labeled as emotionally detached. I had other words for them.

I had embraced a positive thinking philosophy and letting go of the negativity about my parents was important if I was going to be change my life through positive thinking. I opened up about being attacked, but not about the bite and my resulting vampire status.

"I went to where I was assaulted last night. Not late, but it was getting dark." I shared, hoping I sounded more sure of myself than I felt.

Dr. Cresswell made a note while asking, "How did that go for you? What feelings came to the surface?"

I sighed, "Well, sheer terror, for one. But I forced myself to take a little walk around, even spoke to a lady who runs the self-storage place. I didn't stay long, but I managed to walk around for fifteen minutes or so. I don't know how I didn't run away crying. I don't think I want to go back ever again." Which was likely to be inconvenient since Majestic isn't that big of a town.

Of course, I had been back before last night, only I had Rowen, a competent witch, with me that time as we searched for clues about the rogue vampire. And sure enough, we'd encountered the vile vamp. Running into him that time only infuriated him and he broke his usual pattern and moved because we got so close. I wouldn't share that with Dr. Cresswell, she only got the sanitized stripped-down tale.

"How is your assignment to rewrite your childhood going? You stated at your first session you didn't want to become like your parents when you have children. Letting go of the slights and neglect from your parents,Jonathan and Rebekah, is important but also rewriting in your mind your unloving experience with what a healthy childhood would look like for you to draw from is part of the process."

In light of becoming a vampire, I might not have to worry about being the same parent to a child at all.

"It hasn't gotten anywhere, honestly. Maybe I should watch the Waltons or another old show for a positive family to use as my role models."

The therapy session ended too soon. We were going so slowly, but I suppose it was never quick and easy to wade through years of hurt.

I opened the office of My Private Sherlock Investigations even though Mr. Hunter was away still patching up his marriage. At least that's what I thought was happening. He didn't share any of the details. For all I knew, he was grieving an upcoming divorce, or they were on their second honeymoon.

But so long as he continued to accept my work hours and pay me and I kept doing even basic investigator jobs and clients paid, I was fine with the arrangement. I was getting better using the camera with zoom lenses for cheating spouses.

I know the job doesn't sound all positivity and moonbeams, but there were plenty of suffering relationships out there and providing some answers could halt things before further resentment and bitterness settled in or even help reassure an insecure partner of their spouse's fidelity. At least I found a silver lining for those jobs.

I had barely settled in with the minimal lights on in case anyone dropped in when a client breezed in the door. It so rarely happened without an appointment.

She seemed out of place in Majestic with its relaxed everything-lake-resort-motif, whereas she was big-city fashionable and walked as though trained with books on her head. She had perfect skin without blemish and lustrous brown hair with honey highlights and auburn lowlights in a flawless style. Even with my more formal business clothes, I felt downright shabby the instant she sailed through the door.

"I wish to see Mr. Hunter right away regarding a job. I need to hire him immediately."

I smiled, "Mr. Hunter is in the field working an assignment at the moment." I fed her my standard line for the last several weeks. "I can take down the initial information and brief him when he returns." I motioned for her to be seated in a chair facing me on the other side of my desk.

She didn't sit, but perched on the edge and removed a few envelopes from her purse. "I've been receiving these notes." She placed the envelopes on my desk.

I removed the notes with a tissue and went through the notes. They were all on basic copier paper printed out in giant typefaces and in thin envelopes you can purchase anywhere. It was the messages that mattered.

"You are responsible for the suffering of this town, for jobs lost, and families broken. It's all on your head."

"Remember the French Revolution, when the people rose up against the privileged, spoiled, and wealthy and returned power to the working people?"

"Liberty, equality, fraternity, or death; - the last, much the easiest to bestow, O Guillotine!"

"From everyone who has been given much, much will be demanded; and from the one who has been entrusted with much, much more will be asked" (Luke 12:48). You have failed and will be held accountable.

"I will not use a guillotine to bring you to justice. I will look you in the eyes."

The last was the closest to a threat where the others were blowing off steam.

"I gather from these letters that you are part of the Amherst family?" I asked.

The Amhersts didn't have the distinction of founding Majestic, but they practically built it themselves. It was barely a stop on the way to anywhere else when the Amherst family settled in Majestic around the 1850s and opened a sizable manufacturing plant to produce mattresses with the new spring-coil system.

The Amherst Mattress Company was the entire economic engine of the town. Until the family began outsourcing more and more of the work overseas and then they completely shut down the plant in town. Majestic nearly became a ghost town until the town leadership turned the economy around by focusing on our lake as its big attraction to draw tourist dollars. The town was just beginning to thrive after many rough scrabble years.

"Yes, I'm Victoria Amherst. Will that be a problem? Anybody in Mr. Hunter's family impacted by the plant closure that will color his taking this job?" She stared at me, her mouth flattened and her hands clenched in a fist.

"As far as I'm aware, Mr. Hunter's family are all from Portland. I don't believe it will be an issue. But I must ask, have you taken this to the police?"

"I haven't. First, they're a small station and have limited resources for providing protection. Second, I don't want anything slipping into the papers. A leak to the press is to be avoided at all costs. I insist you sign a non-disclosure agreement."

"We would like to at least inform the police that you have received some disturbing letters."

"No, I can't agree to that." She stood to leave, but I waved her back down.

"I didn't say we insisted upon it. But I had to make

sure. We won't share it with anybody." That didn't include if I needed help on the case and enlisted Rowen. He had assisted me in finding a missing child using his witchy powers, and I would probably need his special talents again. Besides, the paranormal community was better than anybody else at keeping secrets.

Victoria Amherst took a breath. "I need Mr. Hunter to start today. I'd like him by this afternoon to provide protection, particularly overnight."

My stomach flip-flopped. I had never left Winston alone all night before. Plus, Mr. Hunter wasn't even in town.

"I'll be taking your case, as Mr. Hunter is fully involved in another case. Don't worry, I can provide security. Often, just having a presence deters further action." At least that is what I had read in the journals Mr. Hunter had tossed about.

I was pretty sure, other than decapitation and a stake to my heart, I could hold my own with most any mundane human. I hadn't ever tested that theory, though. I really needed to get clarification on the finer points such as my new limitations and abilities from Concetta rather than food tolerance. I needed to keep a list of the fine details I had questions about in my new life.

Victoria eyed me as if calculating how much I could do to help. "I'll agree to this until Mr. Hunter is available to take over the job."

Ms. Amherst completed the paperwork and paid the substantial retainer fee. We agreed I would report to her lakeside home mid afternoon and plan on staying a few days.

The building of the Amherst home predated the restrictions on any homes around the lake. Now it was strictly for tourists with campgrounds and water sports areas. The Amherst family owned a substantial plot of land at the northwest end of the lake with a dock. I was a native and never even saw a glimpse of the house, so I looked forward to seeing the property.

But I had a lot of preparation to do before I showed up for security detail.

I made a quick call to Mrs. Maksimowicz to care for Winston in my absence, then I called Courtney, my best friend, to cancel this week's girl's dinner (for her) and a movie. She promised to look in on Winston, too. At this rate, he wouldn't miss me at all with all the attention he was bound to receive.

Before I got too involved with the Amherst case, I wanted to let Rowen know I had a case to work.

I unpinned the enchanted locket that had a white cameo of a woman with curly hair against a light blue background from my blazer and opened it. This was Rowen and my secret untraceable communication device. In case of an emergency, it could be a locating beacon for Rowen to find me. It was a precaution while dealing with the rogue vampire. It activates as soon as I open it, so I sat looking at the gold reflective interior, waiting for Rowen's image to appear. It was a magical Facetime, in a sense.

An image appeared of Rowen, his dark hair wet and unruly, tendrils dangling down his forehead and stubble from not yet shaving that gave him a sexy look. He smiled and my heart skipped a few beats. Surely he knew the effect he had on me. I couldn't help but smile.

"How did your trip out to the rogue's old stomping grounds go? No problems, I hope." He took a towel and rubbed his hair. *Did he only have a towel on?* I focused on answering his question instead of staring at him like a schoolgirl. I was getting warm, but I didn't dare fan myself. How was I getting all hot and bothered as a vampire?

"Uh, no. No problem. I spoke to a lady that runs the self storage out there. I made up a story that I was looking to thank somebody who helped me and she said it was probably a guy by the name of Jack Anderson that worked at the plumbing supply warehouse as night security. The timing's right. He quit just a couple of weeks ago." I looked away from the image of Rowen, now showing bare shoulders. *Oh, have mercy on me.*

I swallowed a few times. "I have a new client and I'll be providing security at the Amherst place out at the lake for a few days. I'll do what I can to keep working on the vampire problem while I'm on this job."

"I'll try to stall Leif if he calls for a progress report. We still need to interrogate that low-life blind date who practically left you on the vamp's doorstep." His smile vanished when he talked about my blind date, but I couldn't tell if it was because the blind date may have been working with the rogue vampire and bringing victims to him, or because he specifically mistreated me. Maybe a little of both.

His expression was stern now. "I think I should confront *Roger* and see what I can get from him. That way, we won't lose any more time while you work your job."

I wanted to reach through the enchanted brooch and kiss him from relief. I never wanted to see Roger Evanson again. The entire night had been horrible and then he pawed at me and wouldn't take no for an answer. I had to elbow him in his delicate bits and walk home, which is how I got attacked. I wouldn't even mind if Rowen got his witch powers on and scared Roger a bit. He deserved that, and much more.

I let out a sigh. "I would really appreciate it. I guess you noticed I've been dragging my feet at the thought of talking to him again."

"No problem. I'll take care of talking to the little sleaze. You shouldn't have to deal with him again." He waited a few beats. "Don't forget to get nourishment before you go on this job, okay? Just call me if you need backup at all. I've got your back."

I wasn't used to such kindness, particularly from a guy. He was such a good one, it renewed my faith in men.

"Thank you Rowen, you are a prince among men." I tried for a light-hearted tone.

"I care about you, Misty. I don't want you hurt by anybody or anything." His whiskey brown eyes looked directly into mine through the enchanted locket with tenderness.

My mind went blank, should I say I care about him? Would that sound too intimate? Was I reading too much into what he meant?

"I feel the same." That was safe. Then, whatever he meant, I was reciprocating. *When did this get so complicated?*

We said our goodbyes, and I called the plumbing supply to follow that lead quickly. I didn't know how long it might take on this job for Victoria Amherst and it was just a phone call. I used the same story of receiving aid late at night and would like to thank the person.

The manager explained, "I'm sorry, but Jack moved on and he didn't leave any forwarding. I had his last check cut and the tax statement for him the next day. He stopped by and picked them up. My understanding was he had a sick father he had to move and provide care for." He sounded transparent, but unable to provide anything more.

Before I ran home to pack a few things and get some liquid nourishment to tide me over, I did a quick internet search on the history of the Amhersts to prepare me. I found a historical writeup on the family that included a controversy involving them I hadn't been aware of before.

They lived on their forty-acres of river front property in their palatial mansion, sent their kids away to private schools, and were rarely witnessed about the town or displayed any interest in the town of Majestic. When they were cutting jobs at the Amherst Mattress factory, they showed no compassion or recognition of the impact it had on families or the town.

That explained why they weren't popular in town at all.

CHAPTER THREE

I had never been to the Amherst home. I'd never even glimpsed it from the lake, although I had seen their boathouse and dock in passing on the lake… from a distance.

I drove around the lake until the turnoff to the Amherst private road with a gate. One of those deals where you drive up to a speaker, push a button and give your name to the voice. The gates were black wrought iron with intricate scrollwork and were easily ten feet high, with little decorative spikes along the top. A stone fence, equally as high, ran off on either side of the gate until swallowed from sight among the trees.

I gave my name to the invisible female at the speaker and after a minute, the gates swung inward.

The private road was tree lined and continued for half a mile or so. The canopy of trees gave way to open air, and the house sat just past the meticulous velvet green stretch of lawn.

The colossal carved golden-stone fountain that sat on the lush grass in front of the mansion and sat with the drive making a "u" around it riveted my attention. It began with the usual wide pool basin at the bottom collecting the water, then three consecutively smaller ornate stone bowls stacked and overflowing. The third bowl had a tall, graceful woman standing in the center and holding up the fourth and topmost bowl with water spraying out the top and pouring down the sides. The woman had the illusion of wearing a gossamer gown that clung to her shapely form. It was magnificent and the most beautiful thing I'd ever seen. As I drove closer, the statue's lovely face had dark stains, as if she were crying. I had to drag my eyes away from the glowing golden stonework and glistening water.

The house stood behind the fountain with a dramatic flare. It was a sprawling three story building in the same glowing golden stone with arched windows and a covered entrance with columns along the front. Impressive was an understatement. It was a statement, presenting such luxurious splendor in a small rural town while removed from where most of the people lived and worked. It said the occupants are better than and separate from the simple folk of Majestic.

I reminded myself I was to provide security and scouted around, evaluating. The grounds were vast, so I would do well to focus on the house itself, unless Victoria planned to be outdoors much. Although this job would be pay well, I was hoping for a quick resolution. The matter dragging on would only increase stress and tension. That might be the letter writer's intention, but somehow I suspected this person had a connection to her and wanted to do her harm in response to some perceived injustice.

I parked my car in front of the house, walked up the stone stairs to the massive carved wooden doors, which were opened after a spell by a maid who waved me in. She was a little shorter than me by a couple of inches and had honey blond long hair she wore in a long braid down her back, bangs, and a nose ring. The braid had a green silk scarf woven through it for a colorful decoration while not getting in the way of her work.

The entrance was as grand as the outer appearance.

In the foyer, a dark wood staircase curved from the left up to the second floor with a bronze wrought-iron railing from the stairs and continuing along the walkway above that looked down on the entry. Directly below the walkway railing and opposite the door was a piano, a grand or baby grand. I couldn't tell which.

But the site that had my mouth open in awe was the massive chandelier hanging from the second story ceiling with three tiers like an upside down layered cake. It had to be seven feet long and graceful, with hundreds of crystals draped and dangling.

I heard high heels click-clacking on the marble floor and turned to see Victoria sweep through an archway from the left, her lush hair bouncing with each step. *Does she practice how to enter a room, or is it taught in some European charm school?* She had changed into another designer dress. I didn't think people dressed-up for dinner anymore.

"Excellent. You're here in time to oversee the security for the party. Caterers will arrive to set up shortly." She let the bombshell drop as though she had told me all about this prior. But this was the first I was hearing of any party. I guess the change of clothes was for the party.

"You hadn't mentioned a party. Under the circumstances, don't you think it would be best to cancel, or at least postpone, until we catch whoever is threatening you?"

"This party has been on calendars for at least four months now and my guests flew into Redmond Regional Airport and are driving here as we speak. I simply can't cancel. You'll just have to ensure we're all safe." She looked at me like it was a command.

I considered the likelihood of these guests being involved in the threats. Those letters were hand delivered and not by a service, so the letter writer was probably a local. That eliminated the arriving guests, at least I think it did, but I was winging it. One or more of them could've arrived early in town with nobody the wiser. But the threats arrived over several weeks, so maybe not as likely after all. The party added more moving parts I couldn't control, which meant opportunities to miss something and a killer strike.

"May I have a list of the guests please so I know who is supposed to be here. Please direct me to the room where the party will be held so I can look it over."

"We're holding it on the back lawn. The tent and chair rental should be here in the next ten minutes to set up. A band will be playing as well. I'll have the guest list and hired help for the party printed out and supplied to you." She motioned to the maid to handle the list then turned and click-clacked away down the hall. Apparently, I was dismissed without another thought.

"I'll reconnoiter the grounds and familiarize myself with the layout." I said to her retreating back. She waved a hand in a dismissive motion.

The maid grabbed my small suitcase and overnight bag. "Follow me and I'll show you to your room in the servants' quarters." I followed her to a separate wing that was plain compared to the rest of the house. The staircase in this wing wasn't rich and glossy and the steps showed wear. The hall had small sconce lights and looked more like an old budget hotel than a mansion, but that's what the servants back in the day got. It was better than the cramped upper floors I'd read about for servants.

I decided to see if the maid would be an ally. "Are there many parties here?"

"Not as many as in the past. Miss Amherst only throws two or three a year, but they are rather grand. This is a smaller gathering with only ten couples."

This just kept getting better. Twenty extra people running around and I'm supposed to keep her safe from an unknown threat at an outdoor gathering. Normally,

I would say I was faced with a *challenge* to put a positive spin on the situation. But honestly, I felt my inexperience acutely, and a bad feeling crept into my bones no matter how I looked for a silver lining in this setup.

"Oh, only ten. Glad she's keeping it intimate. What do you think of the letters?" I ventured, hoping for a little gossip.

She whipped her head around to look at me so fast her long braid swung around to slap her face. "I haven't seen any of the letters, so I couldn't say. All I know is she put all the staff through an interrogation after receiving one and screamed at us after the next. Any letters received after that, she must have kept it to herself." She tossed my overnight bag onto a bed.

My servant's room was small, with enough room for a twin bed, a gray dresser, a gray nightstand, and a small closet. The walls were standard white and ancient wood flooring in a gray. Too much gray for me. Not a single decoration or wall hanging. There was a small window with a gray curtain I pushed aside and found it overlooked a building.

"That's the family garage. It holds ten vehicles. It used to be horse stables, but they converted it as soon as cars were here to stay."

I let the curtain drop back into place, turned from the window, and moved to block the door until I could ask her a few more questions. "So, who is coming to this party?"

"Ms Amherst's ex-husband Finley and his new wife; Finley's son from a previous marriage, Graham, and his girlfriend; Ms. Amherst's sister, Ainsley, and husband Will; two or three girlfriends from college and their husbands and the rest I don't know anything about."

I dropped my voice as if we were confiding secrets. "Isn't that unusual to invite your ex-husband and his son from a prior marriage? I don't know if I could do that." I watched her reaction.

She shrugged and then leaned in with a whisper. "I've only met the ex-husband a couple of times before. They are snippy with each other, but not openly hostile. I can't explain her inviting him and Graham." She took a step closer and whispered, "It seems he cheated with somebody and that's why they split. This was about two years ago, from what I heard."

"How long have you worked here?"

"Only seventeen months and eleven days. Not that I'm counting." She shrugged.

"What about the others? I need to know who'd have the best background information to help me. The person here who would know of any old grudges or such things."

"Sorry, I guess I've been here the longest. The cook was hired three months after me, and the gardener was hired about six months ago. Once a week, a cleaning service comes in with a team of seven to clean."

"How about any of those who left who might have a grudge?"

"I don't think so. They each gave two weeks' notice and left without any anger that I heard about. Everything I know came from them."

"Who is she around the most? Regular visitors who haven't been coming around lately?"

"When she is here, she's in her home-office working. A lot of phone calls, video meetings, and computer work. She travels to the company headquarters for a couple of weeks every two months or so."

"The letters were delivered here. Did you receive them and if so, what do you remember about the courier?"

"I didn't receive them and there wasn't a courier. I remember when I came to work one day there was a large manilla envelope taped to the entry gate. I removed it and gave it to Ms. Amherst. Later that day, she grilled all of us about the letter. I'm guessing that was the first."

I had hoped for a courier service to question, but nothing so easy.

I asked her for a quick tour of the house so I knew what was where and she took pity on me.

There was a library where I wanted to get lost looking at all the old books. *How many were first editions?* A ball room she said was rarely used any longer, a music room with a piano, a game room with entertainment, and an old-fashioned sitting room that had a great view of the back lawn sloping down to the boathouse and the lake.

After she provided the basic tour, I ventured outside. It was beautiful with the rich dark color of the evergreens among the Ash and Big Leaf Maples, with the few orange and russet leaves remaining on the trees. The lake reflected the deep cyan blue of the sky with fluffy clouds. A huge tent was being set up with a long table, probably for the catered food. It was idyllic.

I slipped away to the surrounding trees and, with lightning speed, looked over the perimeter.

The party space was too open and if somebody really wanted to kill her, the easiest would be to paddle in from the lake or hike in, stay among the trees and use a sniper rifle to shoot her from a distance. I may be a vampire, but I didn't think I could prevent that sort of attack.

I returned to the stretch of lawn where everything was getting set up. The maid rushed up to me and handed me a printed list of vendors and guests and rushed away just as quickly. I immediately went through the rental people setting up bistro tables and chairs for cozy conversations and looked over the tent and table for anything suspicious.

I noticed a man pruning a few ornamental bushes

and walked over. He wore jeans, a black short sleeve polo shirt, and work boots that had seen better days.

I introduced myself. "You must be the man in charge of the landscaping. Pretty big job."

He looked me over in a matter-of-fact manner, but then a slow smile bloomed on his face that turned his solemn expression to pleasant, even friendly.

"Kathlyn told me Ms. Amherst hired somebody to oversee the party for trouble. She didn't mention it was a lovely lady." He turned and continued trimming the bush, "Sorry, Ms. Amherst decided at the last minute that the bushes I pruned last week were looking scraggly and needed attention. Everything must be perfect." He didn't sound disgruntled, but I detected a little wounded pride that his work had been doubted.

Kathlyn was the maid who showed me around. I wasn't surprised she spread the word to the other staff, as they needed to know I belonged on the grounds and was here for Ms. Amherst.

"Don't they have electric trimmers rather than the old-school manual shears?" Not that it was important, but the Amhersts had the money for the best of everything.

"Sure do, but Ms. Amherst feels the manual trimming lends itself to more attention to detail rather than rushing through a job. She's the boss."

I really wish being a vampire came with something to detect people's motives, because gardener Ethan Spencer was a puzzle to me. I couldn't tell if he was who he presented himself as or if he had hidden motives.

"I must say I would've expected more of a barroom bouncer than a pretty gal. You don't seem the type to stop a party crasher, let alone a stalker." He smiled but kept cutting with the shrub clippers. His muscles flexed with each snap of the shear's jaws and I realized in his mind he expected somebody who could obviously fight or wrestle better than himself if needed, and I didn't seem brawny enough.

"Let's just say that size and muscle aren't everything. There are small stature people who can take down much bigger people when you have the skills." Which was true, not that I was one of those without my added strength and speed I'd gained with the whole vampire gig.

"Are you some kinda martial arts master or something?"

"Or something." I said, leaving it vague.

"I wouldn't mind you showing me some throws or wrestling moves." The tips of his ears turned red, and I realized he was flirting. I had little experience with the phenomenon and would have completely missed it if not for his blushing ears.

"Not while I'm working this case. You understand."

"Oh sure. Well, uh, let me know if I can help with anything."

"Actually, you can tell me what you think of the threats Ms. Amherst has received. Anybody have issues with her or a grudge?"

"So those letters were threats? I didn't know that's what she was grilling us about. She didn't feel the need to tell us that. I figured it was a stalker like you hear about. I don't know anybody who has a beef with her. Visitors here are drinking her booze and eating her chef prepared fancy food. They pretty much cater to whatever she wants to hear, as far as I can tell."

"Nobody picketing at the front gate or maybe hanging posters about her closing the plant in town? See somebody who could've taped an envelope to the gate?"

"No, nothing like that. Not anymore. I imagine back when the plant was initially closed, but not after all this time. Haven't most people forgotten about her now?"

I left him to finish his trimming of already perfect

shrubs and focused on this unwise party. I had a bad feeling, but all I could do was my best. Why didn't my vampirism come with psychic abilities that would forewarn me what to look out for?

I was as ready as I could be. I had lists with names and checked off the arriving guests and smiled as though I were a store greeter. Finley Kendall, the ex-husband, looked me over from head to toe and poured on the charm until his anorexic new wife, Giselle, elbowed him. I pegged him as a player who married for status and money but never stopped chasing any skirt. The son, Graham, was rude and took offense that I had to check a list, inconveniencing him while his girlfriend, Elana Monroe, held onto his arm and seemed bored. Victoria's sister, Ainsley, showed surprise at the list, her eyebrows drawing together. She was smart and realized something must be wrong, but didn't make a scene about it, which I was grateful for.

The other guests were Austin and Sophie Chesley, Everett and Louise Tanner, Paul and Brooklyn Preston, Marcus and Felicity Ayer, Simon and Emerald Holt, James and Iona Blake, and Conrad and Jessica Fowler. Some had notes next to their names to indicate if they were her college friends.

I finally got everyone on the list of guests checked off and began security duty in earnest. I walked the perimeter, scanning everywhere.

Little bistro tables and chairs were set up around the expansive stone patio. The lawn had a food tent and there were two bars setup with a bartender at each serving wine and mixed drinks. Cornhole, the bean bag toss, had been set up by the bushes, but nobody was interested. Not flashy or upscale enough, I guessed. The band was playing soft rock ballads and the most lively activity was three couples dancing to the music in understated moves.

I began thinking I would make it through this party

without incident when the fire alarm inside the house began its shrill wailing.

I took off running and had to restrain myself not to move as fast as I was capable of and draw unneeded attention. I burst through the patio doors into the sitting room and Kathlyn met me and pointed up the central stairs.

Once I was on the second floor, I saw smoke and flew down the hall, grabbing a fire extinguisher tucked in an alcove. I burst into the room and saw a four-poster bed on fire with luggage sitting around. I flung the luggage out the door as if they were pillows and fiddled with the extinguisher until I got it spraying.

I got the fire out in quick order, but the bed was a charred mess covered in fire repellant.

It felt like ten or fifteen minutes had passed, but Graham came running into the room.

"You're fast! Thank goodness you got here and stopped the fire so quickly. Thank you for getting the luggage out as well." He ran a hand through his hair as he examined the blackened, smoldering mass that had been a mattress.

"You didn't have anything flammable on the bed, did you?" I ventured.

"No, not at all. I don't think I left anything on the bed. I hadn't unpacked either."

A high-pitched scream sounded from outside and we ran to the window. I caught a slight movement near the trees. A sensation of dread ran up my spine as I caught a whiff of blood in the air. My heightened sense of smell for blood could tell from this distance and inside.

I turned away from the window and ran down the stairs and back outside, with Graham behind me. I had to be careful to not drastically out distance him.

The closer I got to the spot where a man stood comforting a woman, both looking at the ground, the more I could tell it was a person on the ground.

"Please don't touch anything and step away slowly." I knew without a doubt this was now a crime scene from the smell of blood hanging so thick in the air I got hungry. I was very grateful I had taken *liquid nourishment* earlier in the day, so I was able to keep my teeth retracted. I whipped out my cell phone and began taking pictures of where everyone was and the two people who had been standing over Victoria Amherst's body.

She lay on the ground with blood all over her head and face, running through her hair. There wasn't any obvious object nearby that might have been a weapon, but I also hadn't heard a gun.

"Please, stand back." I yelled.

I was on the phone to nine-one-one as the guests stood watching like it was a sideshow. They kept creeping closer. I hung up and yelled above all their chatter to back up. My voice came out like a megaphone.

It was only a few short minutes, but it felt like an hour before I could hear the sirens. The EMTs had nothing they could do. It took even longer before Detective Glen Shields made his way through the guests encircling me like a group of ghouls who couldn't drag themselves away from her dead body. There wasn't any crying, but a lot of whispers.

"Hello again, Detective Shields, Misty Summers. We were hired by the victim here because of threatening letters she had been receiving. I asked her to cancel this party, but she insisted on going through with it."

The Detective was of average height, and he was balding except for a fringe of tenacious sandy-brown hair ringing his head that wouldn't give up the fight. He had a well-trimmed natural mustache, and above average alert brown eyes with a hint of kindness. I had taken a photo of the guest list with my cell phone and gave him the physical copy. He nodded and immediately turned. "Sergeant, get these people back and put crime tape around the area. Start taking statements." He handed the Sergeant the guest list.

I told him about the fire in the house and how that distracted me long enough for somebody to kill her. I showed him my photos. He asked that I text them to him right then, and I did so. My head was spinning. Somebody killed Victoria Amherst right under my nose and I had a lawn full of suspects. *If I had been faster... if she had hired us sooner... if I had talked her out of having the party... if only I had done better, maybe she would still be alive.*

Detective Shields must have seen what I was thinking on my face. "Look, Ms. Summers, this was a terrible arrangement to begin with and you can't be everywhere at once. Is Mr. Hunter here?"

"No, he is working a job in Ponderosa-vale. Ms. Amherst had only contracted with us this morning, so I came out to get some preliminary surveillance done when she informed me about the party. We weren't prepared, and she definitely didn't communicate any of this." I ran a hand through my hair, wanting to scream and cry at the same time. How long could I keep up the charade of my doing the work in Mr. Hunter's absence? Worse, did my inexperience contribute to Ms Amherst's death?

"You said she was receiving threatening letters. Did you see them?" He was taking notes in a notepad.

"Yes, I have them at the office in her file. I can get them to you." He nodded at that. "Any idea why she didn't bring this to us?"

"I tried to talk her into letting me turn the letters over to you, but she insisted she didn't want the police to know. She was more concerned about word getting out. I don't think she took them that seriously, more like the person might embarrass the family than be an actual danger."

I swallowed and bowed my head.

He placed a hand on my shoulder and squeezed. "She refused to involve the police, and she had just hired you, plus she refused to take adequate precautions and cancel this party. I don't know if there was any way you could have prevented this tragedy." I was touched that he was trying to make me feel better.

I gave a weak smile in response and nodded. With my increased sense of needing justice, I was going to hunt down whoever killed Victoria. That was a promise.

"Is there a next of kin or husband?"

"The only family member I know of is her sister, Ainsley, who is here." I looked through the milling party-goers and pointed her out to the detective.

She shared the flawless skin of her sister, but her hair was a natural dirty blond with a few sun streaks in a short wash-and-go style.

"Her ex-husband, Finley Kendall, is here with his new wife, Giselle, and the ex's son, Graham, and girl-friend, Elana Monroe, are also here." I pointed them out to the detective as well.

Finley was polished and everything about him screamed more money than sense, from his flashy watch with gemstones glinting to his ironed slacks and leather loafers. The son, Graham, was pudgy and petulant while Elana was quiet but had expensive taste, wearing a stunning sundress and a tennis bracelet with immense round stones that nearly blinded me when they reflected the subdued light.

"What about the staff?" He asked.

I pointed out Kathlyn and Ethan as the only staff visible. They were standing next to the glass doors on the patio, with solemn expressions and furrowed eye-brows. I hadn't met the chef yet and he or she didn't seem to be present. The chef likely had the day off since the party was catered, but I would have to verify that.

"Will you be staying here, or is your commitment fulfilled?" He looked me in the eyes.

I fought to not wring my hands, so I folded them and gripped tight. My legal commitment was over, but my personal commitment wasn't. I also didn't want Mr. Hunter to get any backlash because I took the case in his name and the client was murdered.

"I don't think Mr. Hunter would feel right not following up on this case since Ms. Amherst gave a retainer fee. I don't know about staying on the premises, though. What would you advise?" I would take any guidance I could get.

He nodded as though he appreciated the desire to continue working on the case and asking his professional opinion. "Well, it'd be good to keep you here, even if you don't stay overnight. You know we're a small police force and you helped us out the last time. Particularly considering some of these folks might not leave right away. You can be my eyes and ears."

I could barely believe he wanted me to help with his investigation after what I felt was my failure to protect Victoria. He took my full statement and let me go.

"Can I ask a question?"

He nodded.

"What was the cause of death? I couldn't tell and I didn't want to touch anything."

"We have our patrolman who processes our forensics on the way now. He had to leave a dispute between campers on the lake that sent one to the hospital. I haven't found an obvious weapon and my initial take is head trauma. The doctor who doubles as our medical examiner is currently in surgery, but she'll be here as soon as she can as well." It was a small town with a small police department and thus only a part-time coroner.

"Does this mean you haven't found the murder weapon?"

"Nothing so far. Nothing around the body to account for the head trauma and, nothing with blood on it either." His shoulders slumped a little. I didn't envy him searching all the acreage for something that could have been used to pummel Victoria.

Apart from an absentee murder weapon and the notes referencing the revenge for the Amherst plant closing, there wasn't much. My initial theory is the killer had something to do with the mattress factory that closed in town. But that included most of the town in some way, and that was years ago. Still, you couldn't leave the town destitute and not generate some bitter feelings towards the family. But would a person with that much anger wait years for revenge?

wo officers were wrapping up the interviews with the guests based on my list, noting how long each couple would be staying. That comprised about half of the entire Majestic police force counting the detective. I watched everything, hoping to spot the shadow among the trees or anything suspicious.

Finley stomped up to Detective Shields, but I couldn't hear what he said. A few seconds into their discussion, Finley crossed his arms over his chest and stood with his feet apart, stubborn and rooted.

Detective Shields left him standing there and walked to the center of the guests, cleared his throat and declared loudly, "We're done with initial statements, but forensics will be here for another few hours processing both the bedroom fire and this outdoor area. Additionally, the private investigation firm," he motioned towards me, "will be here as well, according to their schedule. Please provide Ms. Summers and her boss, Mr. Hunter, your full cooperation."

Finley shook a pointed finger at Detective Shields and opened his mouth, but Detective Shields cut him off, "That is final. Ms. Summers stays, and any further complaints about it can be made to my boss. And such a complaint would make it appear the person definitely has something to hide, which wouldn't look good." He glared into Finley's eyes as he said it.

Eyes turned to me and I realized what the term "bug under a microscope" meant and it wasn't pleasant. I imagined a wave of suspicion and dislike directed toward me. This day was certainly *challenging*.

Finley's new wife, Giselle, the anorexic wonder who seemed to buy more hair product than food, edged up to him, placed a hand on his tanned arm, and said a few words in a whisper, "What difference does it make?" Finley let out a huff and stalked off to the house. She followed, wobbling on her designer shoes with red bottoms across the grass.

The forensics patrolman would be busy for a good while yet. I saw Dr. Callaway, the doctor who removed my appendix when I was a teen, doing a preliminary exam as the medical examiner. She stood, tore her gloves off, and swept back several locks of hair that had escaped her bun. She clearly wasn't a vampire because she'd aged from my memory of her. Her hair was mostly gray although kept in a stylish bob and she had a thicker middle than I remembered, but her hazel eyes were sharp.

"Dr. Callaway, I'm Misty, the private investigator hired this morning."

She shook my offered hand with a strong grip. "Nice to meet you. Sorry your job took a tragic turn." She began walking away at a fast clip.

"Um, you probably don't remember me, but you did my appendectomy when I was a teen." I matched her pace.

She stopped and looked me in the eyes, then shook her head, "Sorry, I don't remember you."

"Oh, I didn't expect you would. I'm helping the police on this, and I hoped you had some initial thoughts." Asking couldn't hurt.

"I don't like saying anything until I'm finished with

my complete autopsy. Official autopsy results will be sent to Detective Shields. I'm sure you understand." She nodded as though that settled any further questions and walked to the ME's van.

It was worth a shot to see if she'd share anything. Unless I'm told otherwise, I was proceeding with a blow to the head as the cause of death.

The body was loaded into the van without ceremony. It struck me how sad that was. Her sister or ex-husband weren't there as the body zoomed away, as if she was already forgotten. She may not have been a warm and gregarious person from what I'd witnessed in our short acquaintance, but she deserved her killer caught and brought to trial.

I looked at the few remaining couples milling around the lawn, waiting to give their statements. I strolled over to Graham and his girlfriend as casually as I could. When Graham made eye contact, I moved closer.

"My condolences on your loss, Mr. Kendall."

"Thanks, but she wasn't my mother. She was married to my father, and we weren't close at all." He seemed bored rather than distraught. But he was talking to me and maybe that would encourage others to talk to follow suit.

"Do you know anybody who wanted to kill Victoria?"

He chuckled, "Besides most everyone in this town, from what I've heard? There are many, since she had no concept of others' feelings."

"Can you narrow that down any? More like anybody, *recently*, who was clearly angry with her or had a grudge?"

He stroked his chin, "If I were betting, I would put money on Brooklyn Preston right over there." He pointed to a tanned woman who wore a baby blue halter top and matching flowing flared pants with embedded bling trim. "Yep, the story goes there was bad blood between them from college. Somehow, they still invited each other to events. Probably to one-up each other."

"Was this bad blood enough to kill Miss Amherst over?"

"I believe the rift between them was still active. But, if I ever heard what caused their hard feelings to begin with, it was either lame or I just didn't care at the time because I can't remember why. Maybe you can ask her."

I doubted Brooklyn would share about any falling-out between her and Victoria in light of the murder. I noted on my phone that Graham suspected Brooklyn.

I had planned on staying the night at the Amherst mansion for security, but my focus had changed to investigation now and my presence wasn't needed round-the-clock. But I wanted to keep a presence here. Perhaps I could come and go, because I still had Jack Anderson, villainous vampire, to track down.

I pulled up the photo of the guest list and I made the rounds of the caterers and the band members and noted all their full names and addresses before they all left now that the police had released them.

All of them claimed no personal connection to Victoria, which seemed feasible being service industry and she being Majestic royalty and traveled so much. They all said they were watching the house because of the fire and never noticed Victoria near the edge of the lawn being bashed over the head. But, I might want to check with them myself later and it was easier to have their info rather than go through the detective.

I retreated inside as the guests instinctively sought refuge after the drama. I found Kathlyn, who had led me to my room earlier on the stairway. "Hello again, how're you holding up?" Her eyes had a wide-eyed frightened look

"Honestly, I'm scared spitless. Someone killed her

with all these people around. Nobody's safe. If I didn't need the job so much, I'd quit." Her eyes darted around, every slight noise made her jump.

"The police and I are working hard to find out who did this. Can I ask you some questions?"

She gulped and glanced around. I waved for her to follow me. I led her all the way back to my room and waved her in. "Come into my room. Nobody needs to know you're talking to me." She dashed in and I shut the door. I motioned for her to sit in the straight back chair but she stood.

"I'll try to make this quick. Who has a grudge against Victoria or maybe just doesn't like her?" I sat on the end of the bed and regarded her.

"Besides her ex-husband? I don't know. She was a harsh person, not compassionate or caring of others, which I'd imagine made more enemies than usual. So, pretty much anybody who ever interacted with her could have a grudge. But I don't know of anyone specific."

"You said her ex, Finley. What was that about?" I leaned forward. Was he abusive and the staff knew it?

Kathlyn whispered and leaned towards me in spite of being behind closed doors. "I don't know if it amounts to much, but Finley is the only man who actually lasted long enough to marry her. The prior staff told me their marriage survived for five years and the two barely saw each other, each traveling and doing their own separate things. But whenever they were together, they argued. I think he wanted to be the heir if she didn't marry again or have any kids, which seemed so unlikely. The old staff said that the pre-nup and divorce agreement made sure Finley wouldn't get any inheritance, whether she remained single and childless or otherwise."

On the bright side, the prior staff sure knew a lot about Victoria's private business and that answered some questions for me. I was grateful they passed it along to Kathlyn, but how reliable was any of it? I tucked that away to think about later. It seemed unusual to me, Finley hoping to inherit when Ainsley seemed the natural next in line if there were indeed a pre-nup that disqualified him. Besides, they are divorced now. Who would expect to inherit after a divorce?

"Do you know who inherits everything? That must be a lot of money." I nodded my head to encourage her.

She crossed her arms and leaned forward, "Because of the pre-nup, I'd guess Ainsley gets everything. Victoria didn't seem close to anybody, but Ainsley is her only living close relative."

"Close relative?" I scrunched my eyebrows.

"There may be some aunts, uncles, or distant cousins, that sort of thing. I don't know."

"What about anybody upset over the manufacturing and warehouse closing? Was there anybody who lost their jobs who was unusually angry about it?"

"Unusually angry? Not that I can think of. I remember the whole town wanted to strangle her the first year after she closed it. But that anger died out. I can't think of anyone who is still angry."

"Before the fire in the bedroom, was anybody at all still inside other than yourself? Or anything unusual or out of place?"

She screwed up her mouth in thought, "No. I didn't see anybody. I'm pretty sure all the guests had gone outside. I can't think of anything that seemed unusual." She shrugged her shoulders, "Sorry, I'm not much help."

"What about the guests, have you picked up on any of them seeming to have hard feelings with Ms. Amherst."

She shivered, "No. I haven't picked up anything from them." Her voice dropped to a whisper, "But can ghosts, you know, hurt a person?"

"A ghost? Um, well, I don't really know. Have you seen something...?"

"Oh, the mansion is haunted. We've all seen the woman that died here. She walks the halls still. That's the only unusual thing. But she never seemed murderous to me."

Didn't every house over a hundred years old have a rumored ghost? I doubted a ghost would write threatening letters, let alone seek vengeance over the loss of jobs for the living.

"I can't say about spirits. But are you sure you can't think of anybody else who was unhappy or had a grudge against Ms. Amherst?"

"I guess Finley's son might have resented the prenup if he expected to inherit her fortune someday." She shrugged her shoulders. "The prior staff said he was already spoiled and completely self-absorbed, and with Ms. Amherst being much the same, they had a mutual dislike for each other. I'm sorry I can't help more."

"You've helped, thanks. I probably won't be down for dinner or whatever is happening tonight, I've got work to do. Can you let me know what the guests are saying in their gossip? Oh, and what's the code to the gate so I don't have to bother you?" She told me the entry gate code and agreed she'd keep her ears open for gossip. That would probably be the best intel I would get. She left as soon as it was clear I had asked everything, careful to not be seen.

I unlocked the bedroom side window and exited onto the roof that extended out for a couple of feet. I didn't know how late I would get back and the house would likely be locked up, so this was easier than knocking until somebody let me in. It was easy for me to hang down and drop quickly. I glanced around to ensure nobody was looking. Since this was the servant's wing and only two stories tucked away and the servants lived in town, there wasn't anybody to see me in this wing.

Before I left for my office, I wanted to see if the landscaper, Ethan, was still on site. I zipped through trees for cover and made it around to the ornamental bushes he was trimming earlier. The tents and tables were gone, the guests were inside, and no sign of Ethan. I ducked back into the trees and sped around the employee wing.

The landscaping and planting shed was on the far side of a graveled parking lot, I surmised, was for employees to keep it from sight of the rest of the house. The shed was large with half of it glass-enclosed for seedlings to have sunlight. I could see movement inside. Is it wrong that even in this simple hunt, I felt triumphant for tracking him down? It's important to enjoy your work.

I knocked on the door as I entered. Ethan turned, a seedling bush with bright yellow leaves tinged with red in his hands, the roots in a ball of dirt.

"Hold on a minute, let me finish this." He tucked the shrub's roots into a massive planter sitting in a wheelbarrow half full with rich dark earth. He took trowels of dirt from the wheelbarrow and patted them into the planter until the dirt was an inch from the top, talking to the bush the entire time. "You're doing just fine. You're going to grow up strong and fill out." Watching him was like a parent caring for a child, tucking a youngster into bed.

He grabbed a towel and wiped the dirt from his hands. "How're you doing after Ms. Amherst? That must've been a shock for you." He gave me a concerned look.

It had been my first dead body, and it was permanently etched in my memory. Big, bad, scary vampire, that's me, squeamish at the sight of a dead woman.

I crossed my arms. "It was a shock, sure. I don't remember seeing you again after you were trimming the bushes until the police were here.. It occurred to me you weren't with the guests. Maybe you saw something that could help with the investigation." I thought this was a kinder way to ask where he was at the critical moment.

He put his hands on his hips. "I was right here, preparing to harvest many of the flowering bulbs in the next few weeks. We'll have a hard freeze before long." He tossed the towel, then bent over and picked up the big bag of soil and lugged it into a corner, giving me a look at his muscular arms that wielded enough power to strike Ms. Amherst down. "If it makes a difference, I gave a statement to the officer and the detective. I didn't see anything. I'm in my own world here. It's a great little get away and private. The glassed section with all the seedlings is a nice spot," He spoke as he put the soil in a metal cabinet.

He turned and looked me directly in the eyes, stalking towards me. I felt like a schoolgirl again, wanting to squirm and run away. His invitation for a rendezvous was blatant.

I cleared my throat and gave myself a mental pep talk that I could keep this interrogation on track. "Did you hear anything, somebody nearby walking or running, smell a perfume or after-shave, anything? The fire alarm?"

He stepped closer, and I resisted the urge to back up. I stood my ground, "I know when we talked earlier you couldn't help with anybody who might have hard feelings towards Ms. Amherst, but in light of her cold-blooded murder, please rethink that. Who would have a reason to kill her?"

He was so close I could feel the heat radiating off his body. I forced myself to stare into his eyes with determination. I had to channel my inner Dracula, and I repeated to myself that I had not one itsy-bitsy thing to fear from this mortal.

"To be honest, I had ear buds in and was listening to some music. I didn't even hear the fire alarm, let alone anybody skulking around." He crossed his big arms. "Everybody thinks of the husband, or ex, in this case. But these stinking rich families live in a different world and even the children aren't like you and I." He unfurled his arms and stepped closer, "I wonder about the sister, Ainsley, and what she'd do for the empire to be hers. But it's just conjecture, she hasn't shown any homicidal glares and for sisters they got along better than anybody else in Ms. Amherst's life."

So, he suspected Ainsley rather than Finley.

"What about Finley? Do you think he'll inherit?"

"I think Ms. Amherst wouldn't stand for her ex, because they're divorced, and he isn't blood related. I think Ainsley will get everything, lock, stock, and barrel."

"Have any of the guests seemed suspicious to you? Anybody on the grounds in the last few months who shouldn't be here?"

He gazed intently at me. "Nothing unusual. Would you like a tour of the loveliest areas on the property? We could take a picnic basket of food and a blanket. I promise to have you back by dark… or not."

Last time he flirted, his ears turned red, but not this time. Could this be a ploy to distract more than actual interest? I didn't get any more information from him, other than feeling more uncomfortable. When I finished with Ethan, I took photos of the employee cars and plates with my phone and headed to the office. I'd make a point of talking with the cook tomorrow. He was the only other regular employee who could give me insight into Victoria or anything suspicious around the house.

My Private Sherlock office had become like a

second home to me and I felt comfortable in its coziness and soft lighting. The lake theme decor was kitschy. A canvas of "Lake Rules," some crossed boat oars, some rustic wooden planks painted saying "You're on Lake Time" and the matching "Life is Better at the Lake," dominated the walls around my desk. I didn't care for the seven-foot-long two-man tree saw painted with a scene of Majestic Lake because the artwork was so amateurish, out of proportion, and cheesy. There was a battery operated motion-triggered singing fish hanging on a wooden plaque over the coffeepot. It crooned some country song about cool, clear water. I had removed the batteries shortly after I started. All these things had eventually become comforting to me.

I settled into my desk and looked up the servants' cars. My thinking was to see their registration to get full names for any further searches if needed. Having the full birth name was critical in most cases.

The maid- Kathlyn Parker, the cook-Caleb Naylor, and the gardener- Ethan Spencer. I had photos of Kathlyn and Ethan's cars, but the cook's vehicle wasn't in the lot. I needed to find out if he was still on the property, even though the party was catered. I sat back for a few moments to process my thoughts.

As far as setting the fire and then killing Victoria, all the servants and the guests were suspects, except maybe Graham who ran to the fire just behind me so it didn't seem likely he had time to kill her, too. The band was playing, and they were all on stage at the time, so at this point I wasn't considering them.

I had watched the catering crew during their setup and ensured all but one remained to tend the buffet table and refreshments. As far as I could tell, that young woman had never left the food tent, so I wasn't considering her, but it could all change. The crew who arrived in a truck and set up the tents and food tables came and all left before the party began. I made sure all the rental people left.

I had to consider the possibility of an unknown person or persons who climbed the stone wall somewhere along the vast acreage or maybe slipped from a boat and swam ashore then somehow snuck into the house to set the fire as a distraction and escaped outside without being seen to bludgeon Victoria. That seemed incredibly unlikely, though. The person would need to be unusually fast, like a vampire to set the fire and surreptitiously get outside and surprise Ms. Amherst enough to suddenly kill her.

Or could it have been two people working in tandem? One to set the fire as a distraction and the other to kill Victoria. That seemed more likely, but twice as hard to figure out and to prove. I had my work cut out for me. I had glimpsed what I thought was movement near the treeline behind the body, but I couldn't be sure it wasn't an animal or bird. At that moment, I couldn't zoom off to find out and now there wasn't any trace.

I did an internet search on the Amherst Mattress Factory closing, but only found national news mentions. I would have to go to the local paper and see what they had available. I didn't know if it would be saved digitally or not. I made copies of all the threatening letters and placed the originals in a file folder to drop off with Detective Shields.

I then searched for a college with a history department. I found a few that seemed to have larger history departments and emailed the history department heads, asking if there was a professor I could speak with regarding the French Revolution.

I figured understanding why somebody would reference it might help to track them down. Phone or video conference was my best bet because there weren't any within reasonable driving time. One of the joys of being in a secluded small town. I phoned around and left messages. They must all be in classes at the moment.

I got up to stretch and walk about in the office space. I felt I needed to keep making progress, even if it was small things.

I used my enchanted locket to contact Rowen. It seemed like days since I'd last spoken to him, not this morning. It felt like several minutes passed, but it was hard to tell. There was no ringing like a phone. Finally, Rowen's image appeared in the shiny metal of the inside of the locket, where a photo would typically be placed. His handsome face brightened my spirits immediately.

Rowen was the epitome of European rugged good looks, his sandy brown hair had slight waves that swept back or sometimes, like now, were unruly and dangled over his eyes. His strong jaw sported a slight afternoon shadow. The combination made him look suave, with a hint of a bad boy. My breath left me just looking at him, and I sat down before my legs went weak. His smile lit up his warm chocolate eyes, and I had to struggle to remember why I called him.

"I didn't think I would hear from you until later tonight, when you're tucked in for the night." Somehow, his words made me warm all over.

"Well, it hasn't turned out like I planned or expected." I took a deep breath. "Victoria Amherst was murdered this afternoon right under my nose." I removed my glasses and rubbed the bridge of my nose before putting them back on. I would have bet vampires couldn't cry, but my eyes filled from the sense of failure at doing my job and the resulting loss of life.

"That's going to rock Majestic. It's the biggest news since the plant closed. It's not your fault either."

I took a deep breath and changed the direction of the talk. "You can't say anything to anybody. The police or the family will let the news out when the time is right, but for now, not a word."

"Scout's honor." He gave me a two-fingered scout salute with a twinkle in his eyes. *Did he have any clue the effect he had on me?* I swallowed and gathered my thoughts. Between my sense of failure and my head reeling looking at him, I was a little scattered and had to focus.

I shook my head. "I was hoping to get your help with this. At this point, we don't have the murder weapon. It's something used to bash Amherst's head in, but no idea what it might be."

He stroked his chin. "I think I can at least narrow a search area down to a dozen yards or so at the least, and maybe even better. When and where shall I meet you?"

"I'm thinking tonight, if you're available, that is. I don't know if you need to do a spell or what. We can meet at the office and then go out to the estate. I'm going to drop the threatening notes she received by the police and get an update before then."

made it to the small police station across from the City Hall and the Assessors. The police shared the rustic building with the Fish and Wildlife Department, where you applied for a hunting or fishing license, the game warden's office, the Lake District Management satellite office, and the utilities office.

Inside, I walked up to the window in the wall and asked to see Detective Shields. After a few moments, the door down the hall opened and an officer waved me in. There were only five or so black metal desks with laminate wood tops in an open room. I walked over to the desk with Detective Glen Shields' name plate.

I handed him the notes, each sealed in separate paper bags.

"Oh, thank you for not using plastic. These paper bags are better." He took them out with tweezers and read them quickly. "Well, except for the guillotine reference, they weren't particularly threatening. I'll get them checked for prints and any other evidence."

"I know Ms. Amherst and myself handled them, but I can't say about anyone else."

"We have your prints on file so we can eliminate them." He made a note on the chain of evidence notes.

"Detective, do you have any idea what the murder weapon is yet?"

"Miss Summers, the cursory examination by the ME has barely begun. But, like you, I am eager to know what sort of object we're looking for. Let me call her and see if she knows anything further yet."

After a quick call he hung up. "Not much yet. She has a lot to do yet, but she can say that it wasn't a baseball bat because it appears from the wound to have more angles than smooth. Why are you so interested?"

"I'm going to be looking for the weapon and hoping for some idea of what I'm looking for. Which brings up another question. What do I do if I find something that could be the weapon? Do I bag it and bring it to you?"

"No. Just call me and I'll get the forensics tech out to process it. I'll let him know a call could come in tonight as you are searching for evidence."

I would look at the lake too, since it was so close and a good way to dump incriminating evidence. The lake is rather deep, and I didn't know how Rowen's spell would work if the weapon was dumped in the water. I would have to deal with that if it came up.

"Anything on how the fire started? Anything I can look for in that regard, like gasoline?"

"Unfortunately, the fire investigator from Eugene will be here tomorrow and begin, so we have nothing yet. The room has been sealed with crime scene tape."

"I may be there when the fire investigator arrives. I hope to have something for you by tomorrow on a murder weapon." I hoped Rowen's spell really helped us to locate it, so we have more evidence.

I drove back to the office and had barely settled back at my desk when Rowen entered. He was wearing black denim and a navy blue button-down shirt that accentuated his broad shoulders. My heart skipped a beat at the sight of him. Oh my, he oozed sex-appeal and charisma. The slight shadow of a beard enhanced his strong jawline.

I realized anew how unusual it was that some equally attractive woman did not snatch him up, or in his case perhaps a wealthy lady parading him around on her arm.

He pulled up a chair next to me and leaned over into me. "It's good to see you in person." He then removed a folded piece of paper from his pocket. He smoothed out an aerial view of the Amherst estate and their corner of the lake. "This was the best I could do for a map of the property for the initial spell." He smiled.

"How will this spell work?" I was curious. I was completely unaware of the vampires and witches living among us until I joined their ranks. *Is there a meta census to know our numbers and how many of each variety?*

"I'm keeping it simple. I'm using a pendulum for this." He held up a small quartz crystal point hanging from the end of a chain. "They are typically used to answer questions, but I'm going to use it to point to an area to begin our search."

"Answer questions? How would that work? I don't get it."

"Okay, I'll show you. Do you have a sheet of printer paper I can use?"

I handed him a fresh sheet and he wrote "yes" at the top and bottom, "no" on left and right side, then "maybe" in upper left and lower right, and "rephrase" in upper right and lower left. He took the crystal and let it dangle over the paper.

"I'm going to ask a simple question that has a 'yes' or 'no' answer, and the crystal will give me the answer." He paused for a few seconds. "Okay, for demonstration purposes, what should I ask?"

"I don't know, maybe something about your job…

or maybe your love life." The last part was barely a whisper. I shocked myself that I even said it aloud at all. I glanced at his eyes, and he smiled and winked.

He stated aloud the positions of the answers on the sheet of paper as a declaration. "Now I hold the end of the chain between my thumb and forefinger firmly directly over the paper. I place my elbow on the table so I'm steady." The crystal hung over the center of the paper, not moving. "Should I hire Sabrina as a new dance instructor?"

It seemed like a work question since he owned Moondance Studios. I watched the crystal and gradually it moved and after about a minute, it was swaying left and right. A clear "no."

"Well, I'm surprised. She seemed like a good hire and yet there is something not kosher about her."

"So, how will this help us locate the murder weapon?"

"I will do a simple spell on the pendulum for location rather than answer questions. I'll hang it over the map and it should point an area out. It'll get us in the proximity. That is the first part. Then we go wherever the pendulum directs, and I'll use something else from that point. It's a two-step process."

I certainly didn't have any better ideas, and this sounded like it could work.

Rowen placed the pendulum, crystal and chain both, in a small bowl with salt poured over it. "I'm clearing and cleansing its vibrations now."

Then he took the crystal and chain, held them in his hand while chanting in another language over it. In the dim light of the office, I swore the pendulum glowed.

"Okay, it's now a directional locator."

He placed the map of the Amherst estate and a section of the lake around the boathouse and dock on the table like he had the yes-and-no paper. He held the pendulum in the center "Where is the weapon that was used to kill Victoria Amherst today?"

He slowly moved around the map, but the crystal just dangled without any sign of being directed. Until the crystal moved to the edge of the water and suddenly the crystal pulled loose and landed point down and the crystal stood up on its own in the lake just past the boathouse.

"You can't get any clearer than that."

"Looks like we're going to need a boat for the second part of this plan." I said.

"I know a guy. But I don't want to be swimming in the dark."

"Detective Shields told me the police will need to collect the evidence. The best we can do is mark the area until they can send a diver."

"Okay, we go out on a boat and I get a better lock on the location. We can drop a buoy to mark the spot."

"I'm guessing I'll have to keep a watch on the spot until the police retrieve it so nobody who might catch on to what we're doing can remove the weapon. I just hope there are fingerprints or something on it for all this trouble."

Rowen turned his head to look at me. He was so close our noses almost touched. His eyes looked over my face like a caress. "It's no trouble spending a moonlit evening with you on the lake."

I couldn't think. I just stared into his soft cinnamon brown eyes and warmth spread through me. He blinked, and I pulled myself out of his spell. I'm sure it was a natural attraction and not enhanced by a spell. He simply bewitched me without trying, and that was even more dangerous.

"It'll be twilight soon. I think we should get out on the lake as fast as possible." My voice came out husky and low.

We split up and met at the public dock closest to the Amherst estate in an hour. Rowen arrived in a big truck with a ten-foot outboard motor-boat hauled behind it. Even though I was born and raised in Majestic, I had never dealt with unhitching a boat and getting it into the water. I watched with fascination as Rowen backed the boat trailer down the ramp. I followed his directions and helped to get the boat off the trailer and into the water.

I only got a little wet and found the cool evening breeze off the lake brushing along my skin invigorating. Rowen cranked the engine and stood at the wheel. He slowly motored over to the Amherst dock on the far shore as the sun sank behind the trees surrounding the lake.

I know my sense of sight and hearing were heightened along with strength and speed, but I was in a symphony of leaves rustling in the breeze, birds chirping good night, and water sloshing against the boat.

Rowen slowed to an idle and had me take the wheel while he took out the dowsing rods from his backpack. These dowsing, or divining rods, were two "L" shaped pieces of wire similar to an old clothes hanger in width and weight. He held one "L" in each hand by the short bit, and the long sections came out the top and acted as directional pointers. The rods balanced on his extended index finger so they moved easily on their own.

"I'm going to let the dowsing rods direct us, but to begin, if you could do a grid pattern here." He showed on the map going back and forth in long down-turn-and-back swatches moving gradually closer to shore and the Amherst dock. "I'll give directions as the dowsing rods indicate."

First, he chanted over the rods in another language. I really wanted to ask him what language because it was beautiful in a sing-song cadence as he waved his hand over the rods in a circular motion. We were in the dark as the moon hadn't risen yet and I saw the dowsing rods glow and shimmer when he stopped chanting.

I drove the boat in a winding path like he'd pointed out on the map. Rowen held the rods loose, so they moved freely and his arms extended out from his body. On the first pass back, the rods swung towards shore and he asked me to make a bigger turn before completing the full pass. Following the dowsing rods, we were making our way close to the Amherst shoreline.

The hairs on the back of my neck stood up, and I felt the sense of being watched. I scanned the shoreline and yet again, the trees were hiding somebody. But I couldn't very well abandon Rowen in the middle of the search, swim ashore, and hunt the person down right now.

"Do you feel it? I think we're being watched."

"Oh yes, I feel it. Which means whatever we find, we'll have to guard until the police retrieve it."

The rods indicated we were on the spot.

"I want to make sure there is something down there before bothering the police." I stated as I stood.

Rowen regarded me, "Do you know how vampires and swimming get along?"

He had a point. "Well, I know water doesn't adversely affect me and the cold water is soothing to me, so this won't be freezing to me. I don't think I can die from drowning, so there's that." I still had so much to learn.

"Okay, but don't take any risks. I don't know that I could find you down there if something happened." His eyes had genuine worry.

"I'll be right back." I took my shoes off but kept dressed otherwise.

The water felt deliciously cool as it skimmed over my skin. I didn't have to worry about anybody witnessing my speed, so I kicked and pumped my arms like I was in an Olympic race. I could see in shades of gray, not perfect, but well enough to tell there was all kinds of junk at the bottom.

Even with my eyesight better than an average person, I could have used a little extra light. I swam around in a widening circle and I finally caught a glint off something. I reached out and felt the cool touch of glass. I got my face up close, my nose nearly touching an impressive glass award with a wooden base that I doubted was innocently discarded. I couldn't make out the writing on the brass plate, which must have been what reflected the miniscule light, but I was sure that was what we were searching for.

It couldn't have been in the water long since the wooden base was still perfect. The glass had dangerous angles like a modern sculpture and it looked heavy and deadly. I pointed myself directly up to the surface, kicking strong and fast. I shot out of the water with more thrust than I intended. After I settled back to the water, making barely a sound, I waved my arms and Rowen slowly eased the motorboat next to me and dropped the buoy.

He extended a hand and once I was back on board the boat, I dried off a bit and phoned the police on my cell phone.

I had woken up Detective Shields. "You actually found what you think is the murder weapon?" His groggy voice was incredulous.

"Yes, that's right. It's in the lake within throwing distance of the Amherst boathouse."

"How in the hell did you find it under water and in the dark?" His skeptical tone was evident.

"I'll explain that tomorrow. But I think somebody was watching so I'll be keeping guard. The earliest you can get a diver out here, the better." With any luck, I'd avoid giving an explanation.

His rough voice questioned me further, "Did I hear

you right? You're staying on the water all night until my diver gets there?"

"You heard correctly. I'll be here, waiting."

"Right, okay."

Rowen had brought some snacks and a blanket he wrapped up in. We talked until he slipped into a light sleep. I kept the boat close to the buoy and anytime there was motion, I snapped to full awareness.

A golden eagle landing on the motorboat to look us over was a memory I will cherish. The sky was barely growing lighter. She cocked her head from side to side, hopped closer to me and regarded me with open curiosity about a fellow predator. I smiled, and she dipped her head in greeting and then flew away. Her impressive wingspan only left a *whoosh-whoosh* in the quiet morning.

Fog was still on the water as the sun struggled to bring light to the landscape. It was thick and clingy, wispy fingers that reached out to touch and grab. An irrational thought warned that the fog wasn't normal, like most things around the Amherst family and this land didn't seem normal: the party yesterday for an odd collection of people, the shadow moving in the trees, the fire that sprang up seemingly by itself, the lack of many servants for a property this size.

The droning of a motor boat warned me we'd have company shortly.

I jostled Rowen awake, even though I hated to interrupt his sleep. His movements were stiff, but he smiled at me. I could only imagine in the foggy humidity how unruly my head of curls must look. Probably like those ethereal fingers had snagged and snarled my curls into a medusa's head of snakes.

He looked tired and a few locks of hair hung down in his face, but still movie-star handsome to me. His eyes took in my disheveled clothes and likely wild hair from the swim and humidity.

"You look like an angel with your golden hair and the fog around." His voice was husky.

"The wrong type meta for angelic, but thank you." I whispered, since sound traveled easily on the water and in the fog. I ran my hands over my hair to smooth the curls that were no doubt springing in every direction with no decorum. It was like I was in high school again, wanting to run to the bathroom and check my appearance.

The police boat materialized out of the fog only a few feet from us and cut its engine. Time to get to work. Three people on board and two of them shimmied into wetsuits and slipped into the water with water-resistant flashlights. I watched the lights descend in a slow, macabre dance as they looked for the murder weapon.

The fog was burning off and a few of the Amherst guests had noticed us and walked to the water's edge as well as Kathlyn, the maid, and Ethan Spencer, the gardener. They watched every move and barely shifted. I gave a half-hearted wave to them, mostly to show I was definitely on the case and helping the police.

I suspected it was plain morbid curiosity on their part. They had their hostess struck down in their midst and instead of moving into town, they stayed to be pampered in a house of mourning the loss of its boss, its mistress, its head. From the water, the stone edifice that only yesterday was golden and warm looked gray and dead now. When Victoria was killed, the warmth and life were sucked from it.

I shook my head to dispel the maudlin thoughts. The gloomy fog and isolation of being on the lake all night must be sapping my positive outlook. I tried to find a positive side and smiled at Rowen. He was the positive side. I got to spend time with him and I wasn't alone in investigating.

It took thirty minutes before the divers finally surfaced and handed a plastic bag containing the glass award and lake water to the man on the boat. They also handed over the lights and a camera. I wish I'd had an underwater camera last night. I'd ask Detective Shields if I could at the very least see the award. I felt it might be significant what it was an award for.

The police dive team left, and the shoreline emptied of observers, leaving Rowen and me alone on our boat.

"What's the plan now? Go back to the dock where your car waits or should I let you off at the Amherst dock?"

"I need to go back to the office. I can offer you a coffee if you join me. I know we can't let the rogue vampire case sit for long."

Twenty-five minutes later, I was back at the office putting coffee on to brew for Rowen. I would rather focus on Victoria Amherst's murder, but I'd put off too long working on the rogue vampire who had attacked and turned me as it was.

There was no telling how long the murder case might take, so I needed to make at least some progress on the rogue vampire before Leif started poking his nose into why Rowen and I hadn't made headway.

Although the Meta-Mundane Council had allowed Rowen to assist me with his magic on my cases occasionally, if we caught the rogue vampire and worked on other cases for the Council. I didn't need Leif paying too much attention to us because of the law against the mingling of differing Meta races. I felt it was neanderthal thinking but as the newbie I didn't want to find out the repercussions of disobeying.

Rowen knocked and entered the office as the coffee was dripping and sputtering. He inhaled and smiled. He sat a fast food sack down on my desk and scooted a chair over to join me. I poured Rowen a cup of coffee and added creamer, per his request. I was getting used to people eating in front of me.

Rowen finished his breakfast egg and sausage sandwich and tossed the paper sack and wrappings away in my trash canister.

He rubbed his hands together. "Well, I guess we need to dive back into the bite and run case."

CHAPTER SIX

"*W*ere you able to talk to the horrendous blind date of mine yet?" I was on an arranged date when I was left to walk home and was attacked and bitten. My blind date had been making money relieving guys from their blind date obligations and taking them out himself in exchange for pay. Rowen and I wondered if he got paid to leave some of the dates where the vampire could attack.

Rowen shook his head. "I had called and talked to him. I was supposed to meet him at his job, but he was conveniently not working when I showed up. They wouldn't give me his home address, though."

"You may have to stake him out to corner him. I wonder if he's had a few of his dates or perhaps their families seek him out? I would classify my experience with him as an assault, but other women may not have gotten an elbow to his privates, and he forced himself on them." I shivered at the memory of having to elbow him in his sensitive bits to get away, which led to my walking and getting bit.

Rowen ground his teeth. Would Rowen pay the jerk back for his treatment of unsuspecting women? I didn't want him in trouble, but I wasn't sure I could face the jerk and not sink my teeth into him. My drive for equity and justice was in hyper mode since becoming a vampire and as much as I told myself to put my big girl panties on and go question him, I didn't want to let loose on his sorry self.

Before I'd even thought about it, I blurted, "What if we both stake him out and question him? You can keep me from doing harm to him." Yes, I hoped to never see the jerk ever again, but I didn't want Leif demanding answers and we hadn't gotten any closer. Leif was an unknown factor. I sensed waves of vampire predator power radiate from the man's pores, and I didn't want to experience him angry at me more than I wanted to avoid the jerk blind date.

"Are you going to stop me from harming him, too? So help me, if he says anything to you, I can't be held responsible for wanting to pummel him into the ground."

I smiled innocently. "You don't think I could stop you?" I batted my eyes.

His smile was slow. "Oh, I bet you could take me all right." Then he winked.

My face was flaming hot, but I wasn't sure if vampires blushed, so I tried to act like it didn't fluster me.

He had mercy on me. "I have some time this morning, but I have two dance classes this afternoon. We could try his work again."

That is how, still wearing my clothes from yesterday that had suffered a lake dive and dried in a cramped boat as I wore them, I stood in the alley behind the auto parts store. Roger Evanson, my blind date from hell, worked here, and I was watching the alley in case he tried to slip away from Rowen.

Roger, the man who was the embodiment of everything wrong with the human male, ducked out of the auto part's back door and walked my way while looking over his shoulder at the door as if he were being hunted by a hellhound. I planted myself directly in his path and he ran into me. I'm usually a very pleasant person, but not today. I shoved him off me and he landed on his butt.

"Roger, you scummy sleaze. Imagine running into you." My teeth had grown as soon as my anger had sprung forth. I could hear Rowen racing from the front of the store around the building.

I grabbed Roger's t-shirt and jerked him off the ground. I shoved my face in his. I hoped I looked scary, like horns on my head, but instead he snarled.

"What did you do, send your brother after me? You ungrateful twit, this is the thanks I get for taking you out?"

Before I could respond with a toothy reply, Rowen placed his hand on my shoulder. That was all. I let the sleaze-ball stand on his own, but my fist still held his shirt secure, so he wasn't going anywhere.

"I'm not her brother, or any family member. But I'm a man who thinks ignorant juveniles like you are a disgrace." He took a breath and let it out slowly. "We are going to ask you some questions and we expect your complete cooperation."

"You can go to –" I licked my long canine teeth and made a slurping sound and that stopped his anger dead in its tracks.

I smiled so my teeth were visible. "Where can I find the guy who tells you where to drop your dates off? I have unfinished business with him."

His eyes were big and round and he licked his lips, his gaze never leaving my teeth. He grabbed my fist holding his shirt and attempted to pry my fingers away in vain.

Rowen stepped behind him, sandwiching him, and whispered in his ear, "I'd tell her what she wants to know. You don't want me to interrogate you. There are meaner and stronger predators around than you." He let out a primal growl of a mountain lion that had my hair standing on end. I was impressed, but Roger may have wet himself. He paled and his chin quivered.

"I don't know what you're talking about. Really."

"There have been several attacks, and you seem to be a common element in each of them. That can't be a coincidence." I said, then flashed my pointy teeth again with a biting motion. We didn't have proof of this accusation, but it was a good bet that we were running with.

Rowen leaned into his ear again, "We know his name, we know he worked near the junk yard until recently. How does he contact you?"

"Look, I don't know anything about any attacks. Honestly."

"You knew something was going to happen to your dates when he told you where to kick them out of your truck. You aren't innocent in these attacks." He slipped out of his shirt and tried to turn and run, but Rowen grabbed his arm and jerked him back.

I grabbed a hold of his shoulders. "I think I should get a meal from him before he's killed by his partner in this scam." The thought was actually repulsive to me, but I was trying to break through his defenses and get the truth from him. Besides, after his assaulting me then leaving me to a vampire, I had little sympathy for how scared we made him.

"You freak, get away from me," he whined.

"Do you always insult somebody who holds your pathetic life in her hands? Because there is nobody here to stop me and I'm especially thirsty today. Did you even consider one of your victims would look you up and not take NO for an answer?"

"You can't touch me. He'll find you and you're the one who'll be sorry."

"I don't think you're listening, Roger. I'm trying to find him, so your little threat doesn't scare me. Once you tell me how I can find him, I'll leave you alone. The sooner you talk, the less time I have to drain you." I wiggled my eyebrows up and down.

"I don't know how to contact him anymore. A few weeks ago he seemed to disappear and I haven't heard from him again." He stumbled over his words in such a rush to get them out.

The timing actually coincided with his leaving his job at the plumbing supply, and that was immediately after we had tracked him that far. Maybe he had left town, and we had just pushed the problem on some other unsuspecting town. I didn't want that to be the case. It wouldn"t stop the attacks, just made them somebody else's concern.

Rowen handed him a phone number on a slip of paper. "If you hear from him, you had better call and tell us the where and when of your next rendezvous so we can be there. If there is a single attack in this town and you didn't call, you'll get a hunting party after you. There'll be more than just the two of us."

"If you don't call, I'll get to feast on you. Promise!" *As if*. I couldn't stand being within arm's length of him and there was no way on this earth that I would want his b-negative in my system. Yuck.

We released sleazy Roger. I don't think this close encounter of the paranormal kind reformed him one bit. The best I could hope for was that this talk put the fear of the paranormal, or meta-mundane as we called it, into him.

I was discouraged, a dead end from our only lead. Until the rogue struck again, we were out of avenues to investigate. We walked back to the street where our individual cars were parked.

"I need to get back to the Amherst mansion and you have dance classes to teach." I really didn't want to say goodbye. The last twenty-four hours were tough on me and I was already yearning for Rowen's strength to help me through the shock of seeing Victoria dead.

He gazed into my eyes. "One of these days we'll dance together."

"I don't know how to dance." I avoided his eyes.

"Oh, but I get to show you. That will be just as fun." He chucked my chin with a finger. "I have an idea. I could come by the mansion after my classes. Help you out more."

I glanced around at the people walking and the cars passing, looking for anybody paying attention to the vampire and witch talking. Nobody seemed to look twice at us. "Rowen, you had little sleep last night. As much as I'd like your help and company, I don't want to wear you out." I placed my hand on his cheek. He took my hand and kissed the inside of my wrist. I'd never had a man do that. My heart pounded in response.

He looked in my eyes, "What better place for us to have a few moments where we don't have to worry about a Meta violation. Besides, I don't feel good about you alone with a killer walking freely around there. I may not be a vampire, but I have a few protection spells I can lend to your effort."

"Are you sure there are no Metas around the Amherst property?" I was paranoid when it came to the Meta Mundane Council and their finding out we were purposely ignoring the Inter-Meta-Species law forbidding associating with another meta species outside Council approved arrangements.

We were allowed to work on a few investigation cases together, but we weren't supposed to even be in contact otherwise. I often felt like I was being spied on and it would be a relief to be in a safe space away from any spying eyes.

"I know talk among Metas has been that none have been on the Amherst grounds or in the house, so I'm pretty sure." He smiled. "I'll go get a little nap and teach my dance classes. I can be out to the house this evening and I can help."

I promised to get his name on the gate entry list so he could join me later. We parted, and I returned to the office. I called Detective Shields again to see if there were any new developments so far.

"Detective, Miss Summers here. I'm just calling to see if what the divers recovered this morning was the murder weapon."

"Well, the M.E. has found some hair and skin stuck to the object and was able to confirm that it appears to be Victoria's. She'll be doing more tests to confirm that preliminary opinion. How in the world did you find it so quickly?"

I hesitated to formulate my story. "At the time of the murder, I noted that the lake was close enough it would make a convenient and quick disposal spot. I just followed that hunch. I'm sure some luck was involved, too." I tried for a humble ah-shucks voice, so it appeared I was surprised. I knew this question was going to come up, and I didn't want to be face-to-face with him, so I called rather than stop by.

"I would really appreciate a photo of the murder weapon, if you don't mind. You could simply send it via my email." He didn't think that would be a problem. "I'm headed back to the Amherst place now. I don't suppose the fire inspector from Eugene has been out already and has any findings yet?"

"I know he arrived a few hours ago, but I think he's still working on processing the fire. I don't expect any report for a couple of days at best."

"If he's still there when I return, would it be okay if he gives me his initial thoughts?" I was really hoping for clues. I was surprised how the fire was a diversion and I knew I was pretty fast to get to the fire once the alarm had sounded. But I hadn't seen anybody hot footing it away from the house who could have made it to the back lawn and struck Victoria down.

"No, that isn't the process. I doubt the inspector

would even give me his initial thoughts. We get a formal report that includes lab analysis of ashes to include traces of any accelerant, where the fire started and the direction it traveled, and so forth. That's why it can take some time."

I thanked him and said goodbye. I didn't want to pester him. I checked the messages and found one professor I had left a message for yesterday had returned my call. I called him back immediately.

"Hello Professor Reid, thank you for returning my call. I work at My Sherlock Private Investigations and I was hoping to get some information from you."

"You realize I'm not a forensics or even a psychiatric professor. I don't know how I can help you as a history instructor."

"Confidentially, we have a client receiving threatening letters that mention the French revolution and a guillotine. I needed to better understand why that event was referenced."

"Is the person by any chance of a higher monetary class than the average person in your area?"

"Yes. I can safely say the person being threatened is of the most prominent local family and owned the single largest employer in town."

"Owned? Past tense?"

"The business was outsourced so that most of what was produced locally was created cheaper from foreign workers. The closing of the local manufacturing severely hurt the town and there are still grudges against the family."

"May I read you the text of a few of these letters?" I asked, then shared the pertinent letters from the photos on my phone. "What do you think?"

"Your situation has similarities to the French revolution in a few ways. This will be simplified for your situation, an entire semester can easily be spent on these events and their causes. First, the French East

India Company took over providing goods cheaper than what the French trades people produced, which made the importers a lot of money. But it took a toll on the middle class of France and the economy. There was drought and other factors, but the people were starving and yet the wealthy and influential, as well as the king, still lived lavishly."

"That would correspond to our manufacturing facility closing because of outsourcing overseas for cheaper labor."

"Yes, absolutely. The time was a pressure cooker in France that resulted not just in a political overturn of the monarchy, but the arrest of the king and queen on charges of treason and crimes against the state, resulting in public execution. What followed was called the Reign of Terror, where an estimated seventeen thousand people were executed by beheading with a guillotine over ten months' time in a public square. This is what your letter writer is referring to when he says *he won't use a guillotine*. Those slaughtered were mostly the wealthy, but also anyone of nobility or connections to the king and even many church officials who were corrupt. I can see why your threatening letter writer would latch onto this violent time. If a person blames business decisions based on profit only as having devastated his or her life–and from what you've said, the entire town's economy–the letter writer may think that similar reckoning for their cold-blooded greed is justified." Like so many, I wasn't great at history, but that was chilling.

"I know you aren't a criminal profiler or even a psychologist, but based on the references to such a bloody time period, do you think the letter writer would kill the recipient of the letters?" I had to ask, because the letters may not even be related to the murder or be an intentional misdirection.

Another possibility is that the letter writer hoped to

scare Victoria into changing her ways, although that ship seemed to have well and truly sailed long before the letters. It seemed wild to be threatening somebody with historical references, no matter how horrific that event was, so I questioned the assumption that the letter writer was the killer. It wasn't impossible, though.

"I couldn't say with any certainty, but I've heard of killings for much less dire reasons. As a basis for punishing a person whose actions have severely damaged many families, it can be a compelling justification in the mind of a desperate person, I imagine."

I thanked him for his time. I always thought history was boring, but what Professor Reid had said brought the past alive.

I could understand how thousands of starving and desperate people with no voice and their plight being ignored while others spent money lavishly and extravagantly could drive a person to violence put in the historical context. Particularly as you watched your children waste away in the shadow of parties with champagne and gold plated accessories that the French royalty lived amongst.

That old saying "those who do not learn history are doomed to repeat it" came to my mind. It certainly was a cautionary history lesson.

A looming question rose in my mind. If the letter writer was the killer, would whoever inherited the very same business be in danger, or was Victoria the sole target? Was Victoria the primary person driving the outsourcing of labor and thus closing the local plant, and thus her death was enough? Or could her sister, who might inherit, be in danger the same as Victoria?

Sitting around the office any longer wouldn't accomplish anything, so I locked up and headed back to the Amherst mansion.

he drive from the road to the Amherst mansion was nothing like yesterday. Today, the sky was dark and sullen, a gray base with dark and menacing storm clouds bruising the heavens full of turmoil. The trees lining the drive were looming giants among shifting shadows, watching me drive past with dismal brooding.

Normally, the dreary weather and reprieve from harsh sunlight would give me a surge of positive feelings and energy, but not today. This was soul sucking, heavy, and depressing, as if the entire property was grieving the death of Victoria. Absurd, but that was the emotions I felt swirling around me just like the fog this morning with grasping tendrils.

The house loomed up before me, not glowing gold like before, but shades of forlorn gray. The fountain felt like cascading tears of sadness. A blanket of despair had descended on the property.

Could it just be my vampire sensibilities or could the very land be mourning a murder? Could structures respond to such violence? The house and grounds likely witnessed Victoria grow up and play here, not caring about business decisions but about the people they sheltered and nurtured. I could envision a young

Victoria jumping into the fountain basin and playing in the splashing water and the fountain laughing with delight. But now all was somber.

I parked in the servant's area and located where my room was in the servants' section. It was on the second story and I climbed up easily and through the window I had left unlocked this morning. I didn't want my comings and goings monitored by the houseful of suspects. It seemed like a week had passed when it was only hours. I barely got inside, when the storm let loose its fury with a crash of thunder and a corresponding fork of lightning across the sky.

I watched the storm swirl and gust so that the trees surrounding the house were in a murky, wild dance. This was unusual weather, indeed.

I turned to look at my room and I knew somebody had gone through my things. It was subtle, but I had noted exactly how I had left things, and they shifted enough for me to know.

There wasn't anything out of the ordinary for anyone to find, but they might have noticed there was no purse since I had taken it with me. I tucked it between the mattresses to keep them confused. They didn't need to know where I lived from my driver's license and I would not make it easy to know if I was among them or not. Probably a predator instinct when I really considered it.

I exited my room and softly closed the door. I quietly breezed down the hallway, and then down the staircase thanks to the carpet. I maneuvered through the maze until I was in the foyer. Even here the house seemed gloomy despite of the bright lights from chandeliers, their gleaming crystal dim and sullen.

I met Gisselle exiting a hallway. "This storm has given me a massive headache. I'm going to bed with some pain reliever. The others are just down that hall, second door on the left." She had a tightness around her eyes and a pale cast to her face. I still think she didn't eat enough and was likely malnourished or even iron deficient. Could either give you headaches? It gave me one looking at her pencil thin frame. She needed an intervention with a big hamburger or half a rotisserie chicken.

"Before you leave to rest, do you or Finley have any suspicion who could have killed Victoria?"

She studied me for a few seconds before saying anything. "Because you asked, and frankly nobody ever considers what I may think, I'll tell you. There's an old college *friend* here this weekend named Brooklyn who didn't seem to care for old Vic. Finley said it was some sort of college rivalry, but from the glares she shot at Vic yesterday, it's more than a rivalry."

"Which one is Brooklyn?" Sure, Graham had pointed her out, but I was curious how she would describe the woman.

"Sorry dear, but my head is splitting. I couldn't tell you what she's wearing just now. I'm so sick from this pounding head. I need to go now." She began climbing the grand staircase sweeping up to the left.

"I hope you feel better soon." I called after her. She gave an anemic wave in reply.

Okay, good to know. Graham said it was "bad blood" between them, and Giselle got from Finley it was a "rivalry." Could it be a vendetta rather than a rivalry or bad blood?

What did bad blood even mean? Could Brooklyn hold on to a grudge since college? Why would you attend a party thrown by a person you dislike? I suppose a person might go to a party to gossip behind the host's back, thinking they were getting even somehow. Maybe hoping to see retribution against the rival on the off chance something will shame them while you're in attendance? I shook my head.

So far, there were two votes for Finley by staff, one

for Ainsley, and two for Brooklyn. No real votes for Graham, perhaps nobody thought he would use that much energy. It was interesting Gisselle didn't vent about Victoria, the first wife. But then she probably heard Finley's side of things and wasn't concerned about where his affections were placed.

I went down the hall Gisselle had indicated. I could hear voices coming from behind some doors and I listened in rather than make my presence known by joining them.

"What's this nonsense and where did you get it?" That had to be Finley, the ex-husband.

"Victoria and I grew up with the stories of Jedediah Amherst supposedly killing his wife when he suspected she was cheating on him with the gardener. We heard all about Helene's ghost haunting the house and different servants over the years, claiming to see her in the shadows or objects moving through the air. Victoria swears she saw Helene's ghost. But she was always tormenting me when we were younger, so that could've just been to scare me." I knew that voice was Ainsley, the sister. Her voice was definitely more strained.

"I'll admit the few years we lived here, I thought the shadows sometimes had a life of their own. It was creepy." Graham's younger and rather boozy voice chimed in.

"I've never stayed in a haunted house before. I can't say I've noticed a thing." A young woman's voice interjected. I couldn't tell which of the women it was.

"What does some over-imaginative legend or myth have to do with Vickie's death?" I bet that was one of Victoria's college girlfriends.

"Surely you aren't suggesting that this Helene woman's ghost bashed Victoria's head in?" Finley jumped in. I could imagine him puffed up for a fight like a rooster ready to fight.

"Not the murder, but maybe the fire that created a

distraction. A spirit could do that, couldn't they?" The young woman who was a haunted house virgin asked.

I had to be honest: I didn't even know the answer, and I was a vampire. I needed to ask Rowen about ghosts if he made it through the storm to join me.

"Is this some attempt at campfire ghost stories to entertain during a storm or are you actually trying to scare us?" Said a man whose voice I didn't recognize.

"I only said this house in a storm was spooky and I could see this old place having a ghost or two. It just has that vibe." I was pretty sure that was one of the college friends.

A loud crash and echoing roll of thunder roared from outside to accentuate the point.

I figured I'd lurked at the door enough and strode in with as much confidence as I could muster with twenty pairs of eyes looking me up and down.

They were all in dressy-casual clothes, the men in slacks or khakis with polo or button-down shirts and the ladies in coordinated slacks and tops or comfy but stylish dresses. The room was spacious enough for all twenty to fill the several couches and chairs around a massive carved stone fireplace with a blaze burning.

My eyes took in the polar-bear pelt draped on the floor for a rug and I felt more kinship with that poor bear than with the people staring at me. Ainsley took charge, "Was anything significant found in the lake this morning?"

I took my time and made eye contact with each person before answering. "Possibly. We may have recovered the murder weapon."

"Is that all?" Finley ground out.

"That is significant, for it could have fingerprints." Nobody seemed distressed in the least and their heart rates didn't seem to increase at all, although I couldn't distinguish a beat from its owner in this crowd.

"I followed up on a lead from the threats she had received. I can't speak for the police and what they have made progress on."

"Wait a minute, what threats?" Finley jumped to his feet in a dramatic flair and Ainsley rolled her eyes. I couldn't say if it was from his fighting rooster reaction or his awkward attempt at outrage. To me, he seemed to put on a performance.

Lightning flashed and lit the room like a camera flash, followed shortly by a boom that had everyone in the room jump and the lights flicker.

"A few hours before your arrivals, Victoria hired an investigator because of threatening letters. She didn't want to take these letters to the police and she didn't want to cancel the party. The police now have the letters and are processing them."

Of everyone in the room and their varied reactions, the one who seemed genuinely concerned was Ainsley. Her mouth fell open, and I thought I saw confusion and sorrow in her expression.

"What were these threats? I mean, how bad were they?" Ainsley's voice was tight.

"The last one was a threat while the others were more rants. They seem to be around the factory closure. I don't think she took them seriously or she would've canceled this weekend."

At that moment, Rowen walked in. "Miss Summers, I'm here to assist." His eyes sparkled. "Hello everyone, I'm Mr. Donovan and I'll be here tonight to assist Miss Summers." He nodded his head. He was dry and the only sign he'd been out in the storm was a few raindrops spotting his shirt and his hair looked tussled by the wind, making him alluring.

The women in the group had leaned forward and seemed more awake and interested than even during the party yesterday. The women's interest didn't go unnoticed, for the men stiffened their backs and were sizing him up. I wanted to roll my eyes and shake my head.

"Over this weekend, Mr. Donovan will help with my on-sight continuing investigation."

"Weren't you on the lake this morning in the fog? Part of the search for the weapon." One of Victoria's college friends asked as she looked Rowen over from top to bottom and licked her lips. If he noticed, he didn't show it. Instead, he placed his hand on my back. Was it my imagination that he was signaling we were together? His hand sent a wave of warmth through me and gave me confidence to keep facing this group.

"Yes, Miss Summers and I worked last night and this morning to find the murder weapon in the lake."

Finley stared at Rowen and said, "How did you find it so quickly? It could've been anywhere on this property and nobody even knew what to look for?"

I didn't care for his questions that had a subtle accusation. "Victoria hired a private investigator, not a security outfit. Our investigative methods and equipment are proprietary. I'm sure you can understand that. If you need more, please ask Detective Shields since we've worked together before."

Finley's face turned red. He probably expected me to stumble over myself to answer, but didn't expect me to shut him down. I didn't expect it either. I was the perfect secretary before, too timid to be confrontational. But ever since becoming a vampire, I had more backbone and spunk.

Finley strode up to me and got in my face, "Whatever Victoria hired you for, you failed. Why are you still here?" Rowen stiffened next to me.

"Because Victoria paid me to stay here for a good while, I'm fulfilling that contract and am working in conjunction with the police." I leaned closer to Finley's face, "So I'm going to be here until an arrest is made." I added silently to myself, *or until everybody scatters.*

I turned to Ainsley. "I'd like a word in private with you, please."

My request startled her. "Oh, umm, okay."

She followed me out the door and I motioned to join me as I walked further down the hallway. She followed, with Rowen behind her. I opened a door to find a library and ducked inside. Rowen closed the door behind him. Ainsley sat in a chair and raised her eyebrows in question. I looked Rowen in the eyes and signaled him by placing my hands over my ears. He nodded and began mouthing a spell silently. When he nodded, he had ensured nobody could hear our conversation. I sat in the chair to Ainsley's right, and Rowen stood behind me.

Ainsley looked between us and spoke. "What is this all about? I know nothing about any threats or who would kill my sister."

She was still a suspect, but she could be in danger. "When the factory and warehouse were closed, what happened to all the records?"

Her eyebrows scrunched. "I have no clue. I had nothing to do with the business and wasn't part of the decision to shut down, either."

I tried a different approach. "How about the name of an executive who might know?"

She thought for a moment, "Well, the Vice President of Human Resources was umm… Patricia… no Priscilla. Priscilla umm… Suthers. Yes, Priscilla Suthers. Why?"

"As I mentioned, the threats seemed to reference the factory and warehouse closure, so a list of employees is a good start to investigate."

"But that closure was well over a decade ago. Why would somebody wait that long?"

"Good question, the loss of that job could be blamed for the last many years of hardship and loss. It could be the beginning of a downward trajectory that culminated recently in any number of things, a divorce over the finances, foreclosure on a house, or many other things, but somebody blames it all on that job loss."

"I don't even know if Priscilla stayed local or moved."

"Could such files be stored on the property here? Or perhaps, if we're lucky, there is a digital record that's on an old hard drive or storage device."

"There is an attic and a basement, but I haven't a clue what would be in them." She shrugged.

"Do you know if Victoria was behind the closure personally?"

Ainsley shook her head. "I don't know if she was acting on the advice of the head of her finance department or outside consultants, but ultimately she would've been the one to move ahead and relocate, closing everything here. I would imagine it appeared as if it was all her doing unless you were in the meetings discussing it."

I hesitated to bring up the next topic, but took a deep breath and charged ahead. "Have you received anything like a threat in the last few months?"

"Me? No! Like I said, I've never had anything to do with the business. That was always Victoria and father's realm. She naturally had that business instinct and took to it readily. I was always an artsy child. I got my degree in fine arts. I've had many paintings in shows and sell my acrylics and watercolors under a different name, so they are purchased on their merits, not my family name. In my case, the family name might even hurt sales."

"Who will inherit the business now?" I stared directly into her eyes.

I could tell the instant she realized the weight of what I meant, her eyes suddenly widened. "Oh, my lord! I don't know, but surely it wouldn't be me since

I've had nothing to do with it and wouldn't know the first thing about running the business."

If she was telling the truth, there went a motive for her out the window. She seemed earnest enough, but with murder, you just never could be sure. I couldn't imagine Victoria turning the company over to somebody outside the family. Even if it was an inexperienced sister, it was a blood relative. Could she have bet on Victoria leaving everything to her solely on that? Could she know more about the family business than she was letting on? She wouldn't confess as much as I'd like it to be that easy.

"Are there any aunts, uncles, cousins or such?"

"Father had a brother, but they were estranged since their teens. Some feud over something like a rivalry for a girl's favor or something. I'd only met Uncle Sebastian a couple of times. I don't know if he ever married or had children." She squirmed in the chair. "Do you really think that whoever inherits the business would be in danger?"

That or have a motive to kill.

I leaned forward. "There is always the possibility a distant relative killed to inherit. Have you been contacted by the family attorney yet about the reading of the will?"

"Yes, he is supposed to come by tomorrow afternoon." She rubbed her temples.

"I'd appreciate your permission to attend. I'll stay back out of the way, but it might be important."

She continued to rub her temples. "That shouldn't be a problem, but I'll ask that you not share any of the details with any reporters."

"I'll have to inform Detective Shields, but that's all."

She nodded okay.

That was everything I could think of at the moment, so I thanked her for talking with me and asked her to have Brooklyn join me.

Rowen leaned over and whispered in my ear, "What do you think?" I liked him being so close. But I mustn't read too much into little things. We said we were friends, and I didn't have any solid sign it was anything else. Plenty of hints and wishful thinking on my part.

In answer to Rowen's question, I couldn't tell him I was going on what I'd read in mystery books and watched on television shows. "It's too soon to formulate a hypothesis yet." Ha! It sounded like I knew what I was doing.

"Before you got here, I eavesdropped on them. They were discussing an old murder in the house and there's supposed to be a ghost walking the halls. I was quick to dismiss it, but then I don't really know anymore."

"Yes, there are spirits that haven't *gone to the light.* Those spirits are sometimes glimpsed out of the corner of your eye or occasionally a camera will catch an image that our eyes didn't register. I don't know of any cases with the ability to hit a woman over the head, though. I could be wrong, since I've never studied the topic."

Brooklyn knocked and walked in without waiting. I motioned for her to sit in the leather chair Ainsley had just vacated. Once she settled in the chair, she didn't waste any time.

"What is it you want to ask me? I already gave a statement to the police. There really isn't anything further I can add. I was on the lawn when the fire alarm sounded and I was still there when you came running back out." She tilted her head like a bird. "Were you in track or something because you are quite fast?"

At least she didn't say abnormally fast, inhumanly fast, or something like that.

I smiled. "Did you share with the police that there was some sort of grudge between you and Victoria? That is a nugget of information that they would find interesting."

The color drained from her face. "You can't think that I somehow killed her. That was in college over a boy, ancient history, I assure you. She was probably doing me a favo,r anyway. It isn't something I'd kill her over." She huffed at the end to stess her point.

I mentally noted the situation was over a boy in college. That could only mean, in my mind anyway, that Victoria somehow got Brooklyn's guy in college. Some people would consider that perfect for revenge, but only a sociopath or psychopath would kill over it.

I studied the tanned Brooklyn. She was now wearing a golden autumn sheath dress with low cleavage, but her face showed many lines and her eyes seemed sad. It didn't seem to be the face of a psychopath, not that I had any experience with one. She wasn't dropping me any clues, so I moved on.

"Then who do you think would kill Victoria Amherst?"

She tapped two fingers against her chin, thinking, "Hmm, if I had to guess, I'd say somebody from town when the plant was closed. She had a party shortly after the manufacturing plant closed here and moved elsewhere. When I arrived for the party, there was a picket line at the front gate and a protester threw a glass bottle at my rental car. That truly scared me. She had actual armed guards to man the gate. She didn't cancel the party then, either. I know it's been several years, but she really hurt a lot of people and a party over that weekend probably looked like she was celebrating while Majestic's families had been ripped apart by her hand. At least I can see how it looked. You can't step on people like that and not expect somebody to resent it. I figure somebody from town could've been planning this for a long time." She nodded like a sage, giving wise advice.

I hadn't been aware of a party shortly after the plant had closed. Killing Victoria during this party could have been a statement. It would explain taking such a risk with so many people and out in the open. I'd have to verify her whereabouts when I was occupied with the fire.

"What now?" He held his hand out in an old-fashioned manner to assist me out of my chair. He held my hand and his eyes traveled over me, causing me to swallow and a wave of heat to wash over me. *Oh my.*

Well, well, well, this was what it was like without the danger of the Meta-Mundane Council discovering us. I liked it a lot. He leaned his forehead against mine, "We can't get too distracted."

I wanted to groan, but he was right. I was still on the job and just getting to work together this closely was an unexpected delight. Plus, this dispelled any doubts about how he felt about me. I had been so cautious not to jump to any false conclusions since I'd been disappointed so often in the past. I could barely believe he saw me as more than a friend.

"Yes, we must stay focused." I cleared my throat. "I have a couple of questions for Graham before we move on."

I stepped into the room and asked to talk with Graham. He huffed at me but stepped out into the hall and I closed the door.

"What is so important you had to interrupt my evening?" What a charmer.

"Do you remember Brooklyn's whereabouts when the fire alarm sounded?" I cut to the heart of the matter.

He scowled, but took a few seconds. No doubt it took him a while to connect with his brain through the obvious copious amounts of alcohol he had consumed.

Eventually, a light sparked in his eyes. "Yeah, so she was trying to dance with her husband, who didn't want to be the only couple dancing."

"How about before that? Was she there about twenty or fifteen minutes before that?"

"So she's a suspect?" He was slurring his words, "Let me see, I think she was annoying the others, trying to insert herself into conversations."

"Okay, now for the big question. Did you notice when we returned from the house exactly where she was?"

He stared at me, trying to focus, then his eyes got big. "I don't remember her being there!"

Which could mean she was dumping the murder weapon using the trees around the property to cover her actions, or she simply had ducked inside to use the restroom. Although she said she was outside the entire time. Since Graham and I were preoccupied with the fire, then Victoria, perhaps he wasn't very accurate in his inebriated memory. I couldn't claim she was guilty based on this alone.

I left Graham to return to his girlfriend, who looked disgusted with his drunken state.

I closed the door to the room and turned to Rowen. He took my hand, and we walked down the hallway towards the entry foyer and staircases.

"It's too late to get back to the office and begin a search for Priscilla Suthers. I'd like to search the attic and basement for any records and see what we can find." It wasn't glamorous, but I'd rather have his company than be in those areas alone when there might be a ghost. I wasn't so worried about the murderer, but a ghost was different.

I located Kathlyn, the maid, and asked for directions to the attic. I wasn't sure which would be more likely to have a ghost. The attic was as good of a place to start as any. I followed Kathlyn's instructions and returned to the servants section, and after a right and left and halfway down a hall, there was a nondescript door. Rowen and I looked at each other, then opened it to find the narrow stairway going up. I flipped the light switch just inside and a weak light seemed to fight with the shadows.

We closed the hallway door behind us and climbed the creaky stairs as softly as possible. There was a landing where the stairs turned one-eighty and continued up. We reached another door and my hand trembled a bit as I opened the door. We both pulled out our cell phones and used the flashlight function.

I located the light switch and again a weary light attempted to drive the dark away. Before us was a long narrow space crammed with chests, dressers, racks of old clothes, boxes, hat boxes, discarded paintings and statues, and various objects that I had no idea of their function.

"Well, this is a hoarder's dream." Rowen whispered.

I felt the urge to whisper as well, even though it was unlikely anybody could hear us.

I grabbed his arm. "I swear that shadow moved." I pointed to a spot behind a clothing rack against the wall to the left, where the overhead light barely touched.

CHAPTER EIGHT

He lifted his cell phone flashlight and the harsh light revealed nothing at all. The hair on the back of my neck stood on end and the room seemed to *breathe* around us with a stereo sound of inhale and exhale. My vampire teeth sprang forth. Rowen began chanting a spell in Latin, at least I think it was Latin.

I purposely bared my pointy teeth. "Ghost, meet the undead. Want to dance?" This was my version of whistling through a graveyard at night, being a smartass vampire and bluffing my way through the fear. I could feel Rowen's spell surrounding us in a vibrating swirl of energy. I had a whole new appreciation for his spell-work, and my hackles settled a bit.

A chill draft rustled our hair and the clothes on the rack swayed, then the cold air was gone. The overhead light seemed a bit brighter, and the attic became just a musty, dusty catch-all.

Rowen and I looked into each other's eyes and he gave me a little smile, as if the whole ghostly experience was routine and no big deal. "Thank you, oh witch extraordinaire. Do I call you Dumbledore or Gandalf?" I quipped as I bowed.

"You can call me whatever you want." He gazed into my eyes and winked.

I smiled and gave him a peck on the cheek. "My magnificent Merlin it is."

"Okay, we're looking for files. They may or may not be in boxes. There were a lot of employees, so I'd think there would be hundreds of files. Consider any computer storage device as well." I provided.

We spread out and rummaged through anything that would remotely contain files. There was no hint of anything computer related and no sign of paper files. I picked up a photo album to move it aside, and several newspaper clippings fell onto the floor. I gathered them together to stuff them back into the album when a headline caught my attention: *Amherst Tragedy: Murder or Suicide?*

The article was from 1875, with an overview of Helene's death. The reporter claimed it wasn't clear if Jedediah killed his wife over her affair with a gardener or if the gardener's sudden departure from the area propelled her into a suicidal depression. It even speculated that Jedediah paid off the lover to leave town. Because of a lack of evidence to even bring Jedediah to trial, nothing ever came of the case and there were no charges filed against Jedediah.

Apparently, this angered Majestic's citizens, and there were many accusations that Jedediah had bought his way out of facing justice. The police and judge made statements to the reporter that there was no such pay-off by Mr. Amherst and such baseless accusations were detrimental to the authorities doing their jobs.

The reporter uncovered one tidbit that wasn't explained: Helene had returned from a three month long European trip a few weeks before her death. Helene had taken the trip without her husband and was accompanied by only her personal maid. The article oozed with speculation that she was in exile until a *scandalous situation* was dealt with.

I put the newspaper clipping back into the photo album, closed it, and tucked the album into a box with others. In the article's day and age, most anything a woman did was scandalous, but my bet was on the common practice of her needing to deliver a bastard child away from society's critical eyes.

One thing was clear to me: Helene died tragically and not by accident or natural causes. Could she be haunting the place? If ever there was a set-up for a haunting, Helene's was certainly it.

A few hours later, I was getting antsy to see what was going on with the guests.

We made our way back down the stairway that seemed even narrower than when we trekked up and a sense of relief washed over me once we were in the carpeted hallway. Rowen and I hadn't discussed what happened in the attic. Maybe I'd still have time to talk to him about what he knew of ghosts later.

"I guess we can find the basement tomorrow. I want to monitor the guests."

Rowen rubbed his jaw. "I need to find the kitchen to make a sandwich or something. I'm hungry like crazy."

"How about you get something to eat and I'll call Detective Shields and see what he can tell me on the murder weapon. We can meet in the foyer."

I went to my room and called the police station.

"Detective Shields, I wanted to check in with you. I'm at the Amherst place and will stay overnight. Is there anything in particular you would like me to follow up on?"

"Ms. Summers, thank you for asking. We're going over all the guest's and employee's statements, but it'll take us a little longer to run background checks and such for them all. Just keep your eyes and ears on high alert."

"How about the notes or the recovered murder weapon? Can you tell me anything about those?"

"The only fingerprints on the notes were Victoria's and one too smudged to tell. As for the murder weapon, it is an industry award for the factory and its efficiency. Made of crystal on a wood base. If you can find out where that award would have been in the house, we can look for prints there. But there weren't any prints on the award itself. It probably sat on a shelf and was dusted off and spotless before it was wielded as a weapon. Do you have anything for me?"

"I found out from Ainsley that the last Human Resources manager was Priscilla Suthers. I'm hoping to get my hands on the old employment records to see if one of the last employees could be our note writer. I'm looking for the old employment records from the factory and warehouse around here. I've been through the attic and maybe get to the basement tomorrow."

"I can run some searches and get you an address for Priscilla, but otherwise, going through employees wouldn't be immediately on our radar, especially if they are paper files, since that would be time intensive. If you find them and search through them, that would be a help. Anything else?" Not spending time going through paper files made sense to me, since I knew they were a small cop shop.

"Three things. I heard the guests talking about an old murder or suicide that has everybody talking about a ghost around here. I came across an old newspaper report in the attic about the whole thing. It got me wondering if that old scandal could be rearing its head today. Maybe Helene's family never forgave Jedediah and his progeny for her death. I know it's a long shot."

"I don't know much about that, but I'll see what our old records have and get it to you. What's the second thing?"

"If those threatening notes are from the killer and

the motive is revenge for closing the factory and ware-house and not just to throw us off, I'm concerned the heir to the business will be in danger. I spoke to Ainsley, and she doesn't know what will happen, but she doesn't think the business would go to her since she never showed an interest in it over the years."

"I'll see if we can get any indication from the lawyer, so we have a heads up. I'll let you know."

"Tomorrow the lawyer will read the will with the sister and ex-husband here. Ainsley said it would be okay for me to sit in so long as I only shared the infor-mation with you." We agreed he would wait to hear from me about who inherited, then he hung up before even a goodbye.

I made my way to the foyer, but Rowen wasn't there yet. I wandered around until I found the kitchen. I was surprised to find such a sprawling, sleek kitchen with European touches. I doubted this was the original kitchen location since I had noticed an old dumb-waiter in the dining room during my initial tour from Kathlyn. This didn't have a dumb-waiter and was on the same floor as the dining room.

Rowen sat with a bowl of soup and a thick roast beef sandwich at a round table at a window at the far end of the room. He waved me over to join him.

I passed a man in a full apron over a button-down shirt and jeans rapidly chopping vegetables. He was tall and lanky, with a shock of thick black hair in a man-bun. He never glanced up, but as fast as he was going, it was best he stayed focused on the large knife he wielded. I sat across from Rowen and waited for him to swallow and take a gulp from his drink.

"Caleb, this is fantastic. Best creamy chicken and wild rice soup I've had in my life and the roast beef in this sandwich is incredible." He wiped his mouth of a spot of horseradish sauce. "Caleb, this is Miss Summers, the private detective Ms. Amherst hired.

She's helping the police out. Misty, this is the best chef in all of Majestic, Caleb Naylor."

Caleb left his chopping, wiped his hands, and made his way over to the table. Caleb smiled at Rowen's praise, and I knew he had made a friend. Caleb had pale gray eyes like pewter that I suspected could go from the current bright and happy to stormy gray.

"Pleased to meet you, miss. Can I bring you some soup?" His eyes studied me.

Oh boy, how to tell the chef extraordinaire that I didn't want any of his food without insulting him? "I had a huge lunch, knowing I would be working late. But you are so kind to think of me." I placed a hand over my heart to stress how kind he was.

He crossed his arms. "Private detective, huh? I heard about you out in the boat early this morning. Whatcha find?"

I took my time in answering and gave him an evaluating stare, dead into his eyes. "It appears we found the murder weapon. The police are still processing it." I crossed my arms. "Where were you yesterday afternoon since the event was catered?"

He gave a crooked sneer. "I had the afternoon off, so I was in my apartment in Majestic. No, I have no witnesses. Anything else?"

"Just a few questions. I understand you haven't been employed here long. Do you have any personal connection to the family in any way?"

For a brief moment, surprise flickered in his eyes, but he quickly removed any emotion from his face. "I didn't know Victoria Amherst or her sister before I was hired. I applied through an agency. I had to travel here to cook as a test and was hired. Although private chefs usually live on site, Ms. Amherst was specific that she didn't want that and would give advance notice if I would be required past the usual dinnertime."

His answer was specific to Victoria and Ainsley, but

not other relations. That could mean something. I filed that away in my *curious* file.

"Were you aware of anything out of the ordinary in the last few weeks on the property or in the house?"

"I know she got some sort of letter that she grilled Kathlyn, Ethan, and I about. I think the letters were making her increasingly tense. Otherwise, there isn't anything I was aware of. I'm in my own world either preparing meal plans, shopping for the week, then preparing the meals. I do all my own prep work and clean up for breakfast, lunch, and dinner six days a week. I barely see the maid and gardener and spoke to Miss Amherst once or twice a week about meals."

"Can you think of anyone who wanted to harm Ms. Amherst? Who do you think would have killed her?"

Caleb regarded me for a few moments, his eyes a flat gray. "All I know is what I've been told by Kathlyn since she's been here the longest. Whatever hard feelings may exist between Ms. Amherst and her ex-husband were mostly resolved with the divorce. But they had a stormy marriage and who knows what residual resentments may have lingered. That is my best guess, but I've nothing whatever to back that up."

Rowen had watched this exchange, going between Caleb and me as if it were a tennis match. At this point, he stood. "I'm ready whenever you are." It was obvious I was getting nowhere in my questioning Caleb, so his interruption was fine.

Once we left the kitchen, I whispered. "Did you see how specific he was that he hadn't known Victoria or Ainsley?"

He nodded. "And he seemed startled by the question in the first place."

"That's what I thought, too. What do you think that means?"

"I think you hit a nerve and there must be some sort

of connection between Caleb and somebody in the family."

"For now, we need to listen in on the guests a bit and see if candid conversation gives us any tidbits."

Twilight had snuck up on us. No wonder Rowen had been hungry. We returned to the room I had left the family in hours ago, but they weren't there. Kathlyn, the maid, was preparing fresh wood and tinder in the fireplace. She stood and held her back as she turned.

"They're all in the game room if you want to join them."

"Thanks, we'll do that. By the way, what is the internet password?" I could do some internet searches while everyone slept.

She rattled it off, and I noted it on my phone.

Rowen spoke up. "I, um, I'm staying tonight. Can I have a room near Ms. Summers, if possible?" I raised an eyebrow, and he shrugged his shoulders. "Just to be an extra set of eyes and ears to assist. I know you're more than capable." He winked, and I felt a flutter in my chest. It ought to be illegal to be so handsome and charming at the same time.

I remembered where the game room was, sort of, from my initial tour and led the way. I only had to retrace myself and try again twice, but we finally found it. I stopped Rowen from entering.

"I'm not sure how to proceed. I was eavesdropping before you arrived and I think that's the best way. I suspect they share more gossiping among themselves than if we asked questions. I think if I join them, it will disband the group for the night." I raised an eyebrow as if I were considering something. "Although the ladies seemed interested in you. If you joined them without me, you might charm some information out of them."

"Throwing me to the lionesses already? Is that all I

am to you, a hunk of meat to throw out there?" One side of his mouth quivered with a dry smile.

"I think in this situation it's more cougars and one must use what's available."

"But I'm not available." He leaned into me and whispered in my ear. "I'm quite taken, actually. Additionally, I'm a one-woman man and all that."

"Has anybody said you're too good to be real?" That slipped out of its own accord.

"I'm not perfect by any stretch and I'm very real." He whispered in my ear and I gulped.

"I wish this were a vacation away from the Council and we could just spend time together without having to work."

"Me too, but let's do this and maybe have a little time to ourselves. How do we get info from them? I don't think I'll be any good at torture, just warning you now."

"I wish there were a way to listen in on them. We don't have a stash of listening devices or I would have tried to plant bugs in a few places."

"I have an idea. I can cast a spell on my cell phone so we can listen in. The hard part is planting the phone in the room."

"Remember when we worked on the missing girl before? You did some sort of spell that let you slip into your car with nobody noticing. Can you do that spell long enough to slip the phone into the room?"

"That time it was quite dark, which made the spell work so well. It doesn't make me invisible or anything like that, just puts out a suggestion that my movements are unimportant. *Nothing to see here* sort of thing. The game room will be lit up. It might work if nobody is looking in that direction and for only a few seconds, but I'd have to be very careful. I can't risk getting the phone very close either, because that would certainly give me away."

We agreed it was worth a try. After all, what was the worst that could happen? The killer must know we're investigating already.

Rowen took his cell phone and mine and went to the end of the hallway so he could chant his spell easier. I watched from the corner of my eye as he placed the phones on the floor and circled his hand over the phones while speaking the spell. I noticed a shimmering glow around the phones for a few seconds. He handed me my cell phone.

Rowen opened the game room door. There was a poker table tucked in a corner, a pool table in pristine condition took up a back wall, and a few arcade games of Galaxy and Galaga were in easy view. As if in slow motion, he slowly edged to the left along the wall and out of my field of vision.

The lights seemed to dim in the game room like when a cloud blocks the sun. I could hear a few voices in what seemed a competition of some sort, but I didn't dare look and draw any attention in my direction, in case it should shatter the spell for Rowen. It seemed like five or more minutes had passed before Rowen came back out the door and closed it. In reality, I think it only took him a matter of seconds.

"It worked. Nobody even looked my way. I was able to tuck the phone into a potted plant, hopefully in a way that won't get the phone wet if it gets watered. But it will do the trick for this evening and I can retrieve it later tonight."

I beamed, watching him use his magic to assist me, touched me. It wasn't as if he was showing off like in high school. It was that he honestly wanted to help me and give of his talent, expecting nothing in return.

"Did I imagine the light dimming while you were in there?"

"It was the strangest thing, but I could have sworn the lights dimmed, but nobody else seemed to notice."

He glanced around and rubbed the wall. "Thank you for the assist."

I raised an eyebrow at him, and he shrugged his shoulders. "I think the house, or whatever spirit is here, wants us to find Victoria's killer."

We slipped off to my room and listened to the game room through my cell phone. For the first ten minutes it was a jumble of voices as a group was apparently playing a card game that wasn't poker, another playing a board game with the clatter of dice occasionally, and a few playing pool with the racket of balls crashing into each other. Eventually, the candid talk began.

"I'm getting tired honey, how about we call it a night?" I recognized Ainsley's voice.

"More like you've had too much to drink, again." A man's voice, probably her *honey*.

"Considering the last twenty-four hours, I'd say I deserve to be a little numb."

"It's not as if you and Vicky were close. I remember you hated her growing up." Shot out from a woman whose voice I didn't recognize.

"Brooklyn, you're one to talk. In college you despised her when your fiance ditched you for *Vicky*, and then she tossed him aside a few months later. He didn't return to you after that, either. But you still showed up this weekend, though. I think you wanted to be near her money because you sure didn't care about her personally." Ainsley's voice was icey and no sign of a slurred word. She couldn't have had that much to drink.

Ainsley and her husband must've left from the sound of movement and a door open and closing.

"Well, she sure lashed out at you." A man's cultured voice said.

Brooklyn snapped back. "She had to shift the attention away from herself. I don't buy it. Those two had no familial love whatsoever and Ainsley was always the coddled and spoiled baby girl."

Another male voice with a bit of gravel in his tone spoke up. "Ainsley may have been spoiled. But, that's better than Victoria being devoid of compassion for the economic plight she plunged this entire town into and devastated many families." I looked at Rowen with wide eyes.

That certainly sounded like he could have written the letters. Unfortunately, I didn't know these people by their voices at all and didn't know who that was. I had the list of guests that I had checked against when they arrived, but I couldn't distinguish them apart from their voices.

The conversations after that devolved into snippy comments back and forth, and the game room was empty after a few minutes. I needed to identify the man who disliked Victoria's heartless closure of the factory and Brooklyn could have been getting even with Victoria for stealing her fiance. Stealing a fiance was more serious than just taking a boyfriend. Brooklyn sure downplayed that whole incident. At least I had two suspects to dig into.

My earlier supposition that the guests couldn't be involved with the threatening letters because they were out-of-towners was quickly dismissed. There were ways around that. First thing was to verify they had indeed flown into Redmond Regional Airport just yesterday, or had any of them been in town prior. I wasn't sure how I could check that, but Detective Shields could. I just wish I could do it myself.

"I'm going to slip down and retrieve my cell phone. Want to join me? We could get a dance lesson in with no one the wiser." His smile made my knees weak. He made it more like a teenager going against the parents for a clandestine meeting rather than going against the most powerful vampires, witches, and every other meta.

I opened my bedroom door slowly, and we slipped into the hallway and scurried along, leaving only a whisper of our clothes in the somber quiet. A crash of thunder sent my heart up into my throat, and Rowen's hand clamped over my mouth as I nearly let out a yelp. We wound our way from the servants' area, and I used my flashlight function on my cell phone to guide us. We crept into the foyer and then to the game room. The house was eerie in its silence while the storm raged around us.

The game room was dark and empty, but rather than turn on the lights and perhaps draw attention, I used the flashlight and Rowen grabbed his cell phone and placed it in the back pocket of his jeans.

Rowen looked at the room. "This isn't right for a dance lesson. Let's use the room where we talked to Ainsley." We went down the hall and entered the library.

He found a few candelabras placed around the room, probably for the occasional time when the power might go out, such as on a night like this. With a snap of his fingers, all the candles flared with flame. It bathed the room in soft light, making it a cocoon away from the world. If you ignored the arcade games, it felt like traveling back in time.

His gaze traveled down my form again, and he held out his hands. "How about we waltz?"

This was like a dream, romantic and heady, with a handsome man wanting to dance by candlelight. If only I were wearing something more special. Then I saw her. It had to be Helene, the rumored ghost, in the corner. The translucent woman had her hair in curls and partially swept up, a Victorian dress that was tight above the waist and then flounced out with what must have been several full petticoats. Rowen followed my wide-eyed gaze and stiffened.

We stood looking at her and her at us, then Rowen bowed to Helene and she smiled. It had to be Helene.

"I apologize if we're disturbing you. I was hoping to teach my lady how to dance a waltz." Oh, that's probably what I should've done in the attic instead of my vampire reaction of snarling and flashing my teeth. Okay, politeness with a ghost is a good first step. Noted. See, vampires can be trained. Wait, *his lady*!! My face broke out in the biggest smile of my life and my heart squeezed.

I looked between the ghost and then Rowen with awe. A few months ago I would've run from the room screaming, but since then I have seen magic performed, been around several vampires, a dragon, a gorgon with snake hair, a selkie, a fae, and even a werewolf. Helene's ghost seemed tame by comparison.

CHAPTER NINE

*H*elene seemed to take our presence well. She lifted her arms as if she had a dance partner and the room filled with music. It didn't sound like a recording or even live, but like the memories of a long ago song reaching through time. Helene began moving to the music around the room, oblivious to furniture. There wasn't a sound from the storm, only the music enveloped us.

Rowen showed me the steps and then took me in his arms as he counted the steps for me. "Forward, to the side, and close. Backward, to the side and close. 1 - 2 - 3, 1 - 2 - 3."

We looked into each other's eyes and eventually I was dancing without missteps. I smiled and my heart was singing. I had never gotten to dance at any of the school dances, not that we would have waltzed, but this was worth the wait.

The feeling of being in Rowen's arms was comforting and exhilarating at the same time. His hands seemed hot where he held me. This must be what the term "swept off your feet" is referencing because I felt as if I wasn't touching the ground but floating in his arms.

"Look," Rowen said and nodded toward Helene.

She had a man in her arms dancing with her. He wore rough clothes, not fine material like hers. It had to be the gardener who had won her heart and driven Jedediah into a jealous rage. They each had wide smiles. The candelabra's flames danced higher and brighter, and we two couples danced and danced, lost in our partner's eyes. It was magic. It was magnificent.

Eventually, the rough night on the lake last night and the busy day took its toll. Rowen looked tired, and we left Helene and her gardener to dance in each other's arms. Helene waved goodbye to us. Rowen snapped his fingers and all but two candles went dark. Helene and her dance partner were barely visible as faint glowing lines moving about the room.

At the door to my room, Rowen whispered in my ear *good night* and caressed my cheek.

"As wonderful as being away from the Council's eyes has been, we shouldn't let down our guard too much. I know we don't get many opportunities to be relaxed and free together. Lock your door and if there's any problem, knock on the adjoining wall. I'll be here in seconds."

I caressed his cheek before he left. He was already so dear to me. I relived the dance with Rowen as I lay in bed in my trance-like state.

Detective Shields called me early, snapping me out of my rejuvenation state. There was a dreary light creeping into the room as clouds choked the sun.

"I hope I didn't wake you, but I wanted to touch base before the day got away from me," He blurted out already in a rush.

"No problem. I have some news for you as well." He asked me to go first, so I proceeded, "Apparently one of the guests, an old college acquaintance, may have had a motive for revenge. Victoria had stolen her fiance. It's an acquaintance from college named Brooklyn Preston. She's on the guest list I gave you."

"That is interesting, although she sure waited a long time to take her revenge."

"True, but isn't there a saying that revenge is best served cold? Must be enough of a theme to become so widely claimed." I replied.

"Perhaps. I'll look more closely at her."

I took a breath before continuing. "I also heard one man speak about Victoria's calloused closing of the factory without regard for the local economy, much like in the letters. I'll determine who that was."

"Were you hiding behind a plant or something?" He scoffed.

I produced an amused laugh I didn't feel. "Something like that. Questioning them wasn't getting me anywhere. I could call around and try to determine if any of the guests might have arrived in town before the day of the lawn party, but I doubt I'd get any cooperation without a badge. That would tell us if any of the guests might have been delivering the letters or maybe know somebody in town to be an accomplice."

"Yeah, I'll see what I can do, but it may take a while. I called mostly to give you the phone and address of Priscilla Suthers, the human resources director, when the factory closed. I'm also texting you a photo of that award that was the murder weapon in case that helps with where it was in the house. I'll send out a forensics team if you find where it was taken, although I doubt it'll result in anything. And we finally got some news from the fire inspector. The full report isn't completed yet, but they found a single cigarette likely caused the mattress fire. That is significant, since none of the guests claim they smoke." He had nothing further

He snapped out a "bye" and was gone.

My cell phone pinged with a text containing Ms. Suthers' contact information and pinged again with the photo of the industrial award that bashed Victoria, including its measurements.

The award was part of the puzzle and might have significance. I powered up my laptop while sitting in bed. I did an internet search on Victoria Amherst and industry awards and found a brief article with a photo of Ms. Amherst accepting an award. The hair on the back of my neck prickled when I saw the bulky abstract crystal award with blunt and pointed parts. It was awarded a few years ago for the many years of excellence in industrial innovation.

It seemed a condemnation on Ms. Amherst to bludgeon her with that award when the manufacturing plant's closure had decimated Majestic's economy. The award and the letters all pointed to somebody dolling out payback. But that was potentially hundreds of people. Unless the letters were meant to send the police searching in the wrong direction.

Back on the search results page, I found a curious listing claiming. "Victoria Amherst gets what she deserves!" with a link to a video. The hair on the base of my neck crawled. It might be some blowhard spouting off, but then it could be somebody who was laid off with a grudge and was either the killer or could point me in the killer's direction.

I clicked on the link and right there was a video showing Victoria laying on the ground and a gloved hand holding the bloody award. The nineteen second video had text scroll up with the estimated economic loss to Majestic and hundreds of families that declared bankruptcy or went into foreclosure on their homes. The final words were Luke 12:48 "From everyone who has been given much, much will be demanded; and from the one who has been entrusted with much, much more will be asked."

Whoever had killed Victoria had taken the time to record that short video, thanks to the distraction of the fire no, doubt. The fire in the bedroom was no coincidence, but was it started by the killer or an accomplice?

How did a cigarette start the fire and how did the killer make it from that bedroom outside and kill Victoria with enough time to record that video without me passing him or her along the way?

An internet search revealed that cigarettes were a leading cause of house fires, but the problem in my case was a cigarette could take seconds or up to 30 minutes to cause a fire like what occurred in the bedroom.

When you're counting on that to cause a distraction, it isn't reliable. In that time, the weather could have changed and people gone inside where it was harder to access Victoria or any number of other factors.

Then I remembered a mystery television show I saw that used a cigarette as a clever timer to trigger a fire. It used flash paper that magicians often use. Flash paper is made of a highly flammable substance and is very thin so that one sheet will give a "flash" of flame.

If I remember the show correctly, a strip of this specialty paper was wrapped around the cigarette towards the filter end, which provided fifteen or more minutes before it would set the flash paper off and instantly set the bed ablaze. If you left a sheet of flash paper on the bed too, or something else highly flammable, it would ensure a fire would start quickly.

This would provide time for the killer to calmly get outside and then wait for the distraction to strike Victoria. I remember flash paper left very little behind as well, so it would be hard to detect from minimal traces.

I emailed my theory to Detective Shields rather than try to get him on the phone. I sent him the link of the video as well in hopes they could trace who had posted it. I flagged the email as important before hitting send.

A soft knock had me jump. I shook my head at how jittery I was and padded barefoot over to the door. I opened to see Rowen smiling at me. He looked me over from head to toe and I realized I was in my vampire themed pajamas from a popular vampire television show.

I cleared my throat. "This is my attempt to embrace things." Never mind that the actor was scorching good looking.

"I guess if I have to be jealous, a fictional character is better than the alternative."

"No reason to be jealous. I'm dealing with all the changes, even if some are a tad juvenile." I stood on tiptoe and kissed him on the cheek, then whispered in his ear. "I'll take the waltzing wizard any day, all day."

I stood flat on the floor looking up at him and he played with one of my stray blond curls. "I hate to leave, but a dance instructor called in sick, so I have to cover. I'll try to be back tonight." He hesitated a few seconds before adding. "Leif texted me asking about progress on the rogue vampire. I've a feeling we need to give that some attention before he stops us from working together."

And my day just plummeted to difficult status. Leif was the Vampire representative on the Meta-Mundane Council and was cracking the whip on our search for the rogue vampire who had turned me and a few others against universal Meta rules.

"Okay, I'll give some thought to what we might do next and call you. Maybe tonight we can work on the big bad vampire case."

He kissed my hand and my knees became wobbly. Sadly, that was all the goodbye I got, and he was gone.

I had a full day ahead of me. The basement still needed searching for employee records, I needed to find where the murder weapon had been in the house, meet with Priscilla Suthers and try to get the last employee list, the will was going to be read, then there was coming up with a plan for the rogue vampire. At some point, I would like to go home and see Winston, and I needed to talk to my bestie, Courtney, for my own sanity.

If I had to prioritize my tasks, I felt Priscilla was a better shot than searching the basement for employee records. I could ask Kathlyn, the maid, if she knew where the award had been in the house and save some time that way. Talking to Kathlyn just might be useful in other ways, too.

It was just after seven-thirty and still gloomy out. I dressed and went in search of Kathlyn near the dining room. I found her cleaning out a fireplace and setting new firewood.

"Good morning Kathlyn. I'm surprised by the old wood fireplaces." I smiled, trying to put her at ease.

"Oh, it's only for a few of the rooms. The master bedroom and more private areas have gas. I think these are to keep the romance of the original building alive." She smiled back.

"The murder weapon was retrieved from the lake yesterday morning. I was hoping you could help me out with some information on it."

"Oh, I don't know anything about any weapons."

"No, it was an award given to Victoria and I'm trying to determine where it was kept in the house. Do you think you can look at it and see if you recognize it?"

She gulped. "I don't want to see it. No, thank you."

I shook my head. "It's just a photo, and it's all clean. Nothing to it, really."

She finally gave in and looked at the photo Detective Shields sent me. She bit her lip while she looked at it.

"She has a spot with a few awards and stuff in her private office here, but I don't know if it was one of them. I didn't go in that room often."

Kathlyn ushered me to Victoria Amherst's private office just off her bedroom. It wasn't locked, and we walked right in. She pointed to a bookshelf behind the desk that had an entire shelf for trophies and awards.

I studied them carefully. Most of the awards were from Victoria's early years when she was competing in horse jumping events. Then there were some academic awards for debate competitions. There was a gap between some awards.

I pulled a step stool over so I could take a better look. There wasn't any dust since the house was cleaned regularly, but according to the measurements, the deadly award probably came from here.

I asked Kathlyn. "Do you remember what would've been here?"

She shook her head no. "I really couldn't say. I didn't pay much attention, honestly."

"Is the door always left unlocked?"

"I've only been in here when Miss Amherst was working here, so I don't know."

"I have to contact the police and they'll send a forensics team out. Can you show them in here and this spot?"

She nodded, but her wide eyes and multiple gulps told me the whole thing was upsetting to her. I imagine it would unnerve me if my employer was murdered on the property in broad daylight.

I left message for the Detective and texted him a quick photo of the shelf before leaving.

Kathlyn turned to me in the hall. "May I ask you a question about the man you're working with?" Her face turned a deep pink shade.

"Okay, what about him?"

"Are you two dating?" She studied the floor.

I hated to mislead her, but absolutely nobody was to know Rowen and I were more than forced to work together. I really didn't want to find out what the Council would do to either of us. My imagination had gone wild on various punishments from restricting us with a magic spell from seeing each other again to the worst being a slow death and everything in between.

"No, we aren't dating. He helps me out on occasion." It was hard to even say the words because I was getting attached to him, deeply. The sight of him made my stomach flip and my heart race.

"He is yummy, and I just wondered. Is he an investigator too?"

"No, he owns Moondance studio. He teaches dance lessons."

I didn't think it was possible, but her gaze became even more dreamy, as she no doubt imagined dancing with Rowen. I knew what she was going through, because the first time I saw him gliding around the dance floor with a student, it was like a scene from a movie. After last night's waltz, the most romantic experience of my life thus far, I knew I would always cherish that memory. Rowen was charming and suave, but above all, he was so kind to me.

"May I ask you a few questions?" She nodded. "I overheard Ainsley say that one of Victoria's college friends had lost her fiance to Victoria. Do you know which guest that was?" It was an easy question since I knew it was Brooklyn and this would just get the ball rolling.

She thought a few moments, then answered. "I think that'd be Brooklyn from a few snippets of conversation I've heard. She has made a few snide comments about Victoria having taken what wasn't hers and such. I wondered if it was over a man."

Brooklyn still brought it up, so she wasn't over it. Perfect, that helped quite a bit.

"Have you heard one of the men say anything about Victoria and the closing of the manufacturing facility? I overheard a man but couldn't tell from the voice who it was. It was a bit of a gravelly voice, though."

"You've overheard a good bit, it seems." Her eyebrows raised.

"Well, they don't speak freely around me as they do you. If I'm going to help the police, I have to be creative."

She nodded her head. "I don't know about any of the guys saying anything like that, but Austin has a rough and scratchy kind of voice."

Excellent, because Austin seemed to be of the same mind as the letter writer. The good detective could look at the guest list I provided him and check him out. I wanted to do a little victory dance for even this little tidbit.

Austin was a lead, but nobody had pointed to him and I got the impression he was just a husband to one of the college friends. Unless Austin was somehow related to the plant closure, he seemed less and less likely the more I thought about it. The entire case was like clawing my way up a smooth wall.

Detective Shields texted he was sending a forensics team. I texted back that Austin was the guest I overheard. He replied with a thumbs up emoji. That didn't tell me if he would check him out or not.

Back in my room, I phoned the number for Priscilla Suthers and felt I was on a roll when she answered on the third ring. I explained who I was and how I was assisting the police. She agreed to talk with me in a couple of hours.

Before I met with Priscilla, I wanted to spend a little time on the rogue vampire. I really needed to think of him as Jack Anderson. I had to figure out how we could pick up his trail.

hen Rowen and I began looking for Jack, we weren't sure what we were up against. We had discovered a few tidbits, but we still didn't really know what vampire Jack Anderson was capable of or how he would fight back. I still didn't know Jack, no pun intended. I felt I needed to talk to Concetta, my tutor on all things vampire, but naturally she wasn't answering her phone during the day so I left a message.

When Majestic is basking in bright sunshine, I feel like I'm pushing a rock uphill just to get up. But I really enjoyed working for My Private Sherlock Investigations, so I made the sacrifice and toughed it through the sunny days.

Of course, it is easier with my boss gone from the office dealing with a failing marriage and leaving everything in my hands. The sticky part is I'm not an actual licensed investigator. I was Mr. Hunter's secretary, then I got bit and Mr. Hunter followed his wife out of town to work on their marriage.

So I'm new at the whole investigative side, but let's face it, a vampire doing the investigation when things are dicey is a plus. You add to that a bona fide witch to sling a few spells to help where my skills are lacking and we do okay.

As far as investigating the vampire Jack Anderson, I was starting over since he had quit his job and moved. For all I knew, he didn't want the hassle of the Meta-Mundane Council telling him he couldn't attack people and turn them into vampires and left town. But Rowen and I had to exhaust every possibility and stop him from turning anybody else if he was still in town.

I was just brainstorming ideas on tracking vampire Jack down when my cell phone rang. Oh no! It was Lief calling. Lief frightened me. He seemed cold and lacking in any emotion. My hello was hesitant, at best. The temporary bedroom seemed to shrink in on me the moment I saw Lief's name on the caller ID.

"Lief, I'm working on the vampire. Really, I am."

"Misty, I appreciate that." His tone was dry and not appreciative in the least. "So, what progress have you made?"

"Well, I found he'd been working at a plumbing supply, going by the name Jack Anderson, but when I followed up with the plumbing supply, he'd given notice and claimed he moved with no forwarding."

"Nothing more since then?"

"No, I believe Rowen is going to have to help me with some magic to get us moving again. I'll speak with him about it and what spell would be the best option."

"Okay, you talk to *Mr. Donovan*, but hurry it up." It was silent on the line.

Whenever Leif was so closemouthed, I worried. My mind cast around, desperate to latch onto something else to track the rogue. I felt as if the air were sucked out of the room.

"Could I speak to the other victims of this rogue vampire? Something may surface that gives us a clue about him."

"I'll let them know to cooperate with you and I'll send their contact information."

Another silence stretched out on the phone. I could

imagine Leif sitting in an office chair with a *going into battle* look on his face.

"Is there something else?" I ventured.

"Actually, yes there is. Remember when I introduced you to a few male vampires at the last meeting?"

Uh oh, I didn't like where this was headed. The last time we met over the worst of vampire Jack's brazen attacks, Lief had made an awkward and obvious statement when he introduced me to three male vampires. We all knew he was trying to get me to date one of them, so we chatted for a few moments and went our separate ways. I'd already met Rowen and liked him whether or not he was a witch.

"Yes, I remember." I wasn't offering my thoughts, for this was dangerous ground. *Oh crap.*

"Since you haven't furthered a relationship with any of them, I'm wondering if we can meet to discuss this."

Geez, Louise! No pressure there. My mouth was instantly as dry as the Sahara desert.

"I'm sure you're aware I'm dealing with a murder, as well as this rogue vampire problem. I'm in no rush for a relationship when I'm adjusting to the vicissitudes that have already occurred." I love interjecting that word. It throws many people off. "I've gone through a radical life change and it can be very stressful, so I'm focusing on myself before a relationship." There. I thought that was forthright and firm without telling him what he could do with his throwing vampire guys at me.

"I've lived for over four hundred years, and what you need is a male to guide you." He said in a clipped tone.

"Maybe if we were living in the 1600s, but thankfully my fluttering little mind knows what I need to make the adjustment without a guy at all. You do realize women are more than capable all by our little selves." He was infuriating.

"I'll expect you tonight at my place at seven." With

that, he hung up. I didn't know where the frick he lived, and I didn't want to know either. I paced back and forth in my room muttering to myself with words like neanderthal, chauvinist, mansplainer, domineering, and sexist.

I was turning over how I could deal with his attitude. This was completely unacceptable. The scary thing was how new I was to all of this. I discarded the idea of contacting Rowen via the enchanted locket until I'd calmed down. But Concetta could help me. She was very much her own woman. That is why I left a second message for her in which I sounded like an outraged yet nervous newbie imploring her to accompany me to Lief's house.

This was bad, and I wasn't one for handling conflict. Is that a first for a vampire?

Naturally I had to wait to hear from Concetta no matter how anxious I was, but in the meantime I had the appointment with Priscilla Suthers.

The rain had stopped and left even more deep yellow and russet leaves scattered around, making the streets and lawns look dappled with gold and garnets. It was still overcast and gloomy, which fit my mood perfectly as I continued to stew over Lief's antiquated attitudes and demand for my attendance at his house.

The arrogance of the guy. I was very busy with my job plus looking for Jack the rogue, but no, I must drop everything because he thinks I need some man to manage me. The nerve, the gall of his archaic attitudes!

Priscilla Suthers lived in perhaps the oldest section of Majestic, which was good and bad. Some of the homes had been maintained well, but there were others that the mattress factory closure had caused them to sit empty even now. Priscilla was in one of the lucky homes.

It was a simple cottage, light blue single story with a covered porch and wood siding plus a small flower garden and picket fence around it. It was small town Americana personified. Small but solid.

Priscilla Suthers answered and ushered me into her compact living room that was minimalist out of necessity, for there wasn't much space. I sat on the loveseat and she sat in a coordinating chair. She looked like a photo I saw once of a chicken with wild feathers standing up on its head. Her wispy hair stuck out all over, and she had a sharp nose.

She invited me in and we sat at her kitchen table. "I understand you're working with the police. I spoke to a Detective Shields, and he confirmed you're assisting the police. He asked that I give you my full cooperation. So what is it you're looking for?"

"I'm trying to find employees that may have been so upset over the closing of the factory and warehouse that one may have become violent."

She swept her hands over the tabletop. "Well, they started layoffs a year before the actual closure of the manufacturing side. There were several that were furious at each round of layoffs." She ran her hands over her face. "We had entire families working there: mother, father, and all working age children. We even had three generations of one family. It was devastating. The employees were like an extended family. Several of the children of employees met at company functions and got married. The closure was widely considered a betrayal, not just a business move." She gazed off into the distance, remembering better days.

"Are you telling me there aren't just a few who could've turned violent?"

"That's what I'm saying."

"Do you still keep in touch with any of them?"

"Oh, I get a few hundred holiday cards every year and I send out about the same." She gave a wistful flash of a smile.

I leaned closer towards her. "Can you think of

anyone who would have a strong anger this long after the closure? Because that's what I'm having the hardest time understanding. Indications are revenge was a motive in Victoria's murder, but why wait fifteen years after the fact? Unless something happened now that they blame on the closure but it took this long to impact them. Maybe a bankruptcy or death of a loved one that a person blames it all began when they lost their job."

"Certainly nobody or nothing I can think of at the moment. I'm sorry." She was polite and gave every sign of being helpful, but I sensed she didn't like Victoria much, either. Those hundreds of Xmas cards to and from past employees were a big warning. Surely, if somebody was still angry she would have some hint with how she had stayed in communication with so many.

I leaned back in the chair. "Where are all the employee records from when everything closed down? A list of the employees and their files might provide some insights or leads."

"At the beginning of the layoffs, we had a full staff of nine hundred and sixty-five employees. That's a lot of files, plus we had to keep nine years of back records by law. There is a storage unit where everything is stored. After talking to the detective, I contacted the attorney that handles the storage unit. I went there earlier and brought back as many boxes as I could find from the last year, when most of the layoffs were taking place."

She showed me to a spare bedroom that had boxes stacked along one wall.

"I don't suppose anything was kept digitally?" My voice sounded weary just looking at the boxes.

"If the factory had stayed open, we were looking at my department becoming more computerized, but that had been put off over the years. When they outsourced the work, they didn't have to worry about any employees and their records any more. I know this makes your job harder." She shrugged her shoulders and gave a regretful smile.

"Please think back on those last weeks. Maybe talk to some of those you've kept in touch with and see if anybody has any recollections of a very disgruntled person. Better yet, anybody who recently had an emotional and financial blow somehow related to the closure. You have my contact info. Just call me."

It took me a while of trekking back and forth to load all the boxes into my car, like a three-dimensional puzzle cramming boxes in every possible space and re-arranging. That was definitely the most my car had ever carried and I wouldn't be able to see out the back rearview either. I took a photo to show Lief what I was bogged down with on my day job, not that it would deter him.

I got into my car and I debated with myself over taking the records back to the Amherst mansion. The boxes would sit in my bedroom, but I doubted they would be safe from tampering, even if I locked the door.

My cell phone rang in my purse. I pulled over and answered my best friend since high school, Courtney. We normally got together once a week but because Victoria Amherst's job dropped in my lap, we had to cancel movie night this week. I was missing the girl time since I had confided in her of my vampire status and could be myself with her.

"Hey girlfriend! I thought I would check in and see if we could snag a quick lunch and catch up." She sounded like she was walking to her car as she talked. I could hear cars around her.

"A quick break is all I can really do. Where should I meet you?"

She wanted the only Mexican food place in town. I

turned the car around and was pulling in as she was getting out of her car.

We hugged, and I felt like it had been years since we last spent time together. She normally wore her long hair in a braid, but today she had it in a banana clip, so it draped down a little at the back. She is blessed with a high metabolism, so she stays trim. She has big bright blue eyes, what is called a button nose, and a big grin.

We sat at a table in lovely hand carved Pueblo style chairs that were brightly painted with sunflowers and Macaw on each chair back. The restaurant had murals on each wall of a Spanish village with donkeys and villagers. Once Courtney got her fish tacos order placed, she got down to business.

"Tell me all about the Amherst mansion, girl. Is it a creepy old house or a luxurious palace? Are there any good looking single rich men at the party who are dying for a hardworking bookkeeper? Can you sneak me in to tour the place?"

She finally stopped to take a breath, and I leaned in and she joined me. "The news isn't out yet but..." I placed my hand over her mouth, "Victoria Amherst was killed." She emitted a muffled cry behind my hand. "You can't tell a single soul. Nod if you understand." She nodded, and I took my hand away.

She whispered while looking at people around her like there were spies everywhere, "Do you know who did it yet?"

"I'm working on it. I have a full slate of suspects from her ex-husband, her sister who'll likely inherit most everything, an old college rival, another guest, or the three employees. Plus, anybody who was working at the mattress factory when it closed. So, a few hundred people."

"You told me about the threatening letters when you canceled movie night. So is Rowen helping you?" Her eyebrows danced.

I sighed. "That's another problem."

"I'll take that problem off your hands, in the name of our friendship." She smiled and took a big bite of taco.

I shared about Leif demanding my presence at his house tonight and his archaic attitudes.

"Uh oh, that doesn't sound good. Oh Misty, you find a great guy and your new situation has set you up with forbidden love. If we were in high school, I would think it was romantic, but I know this isn't fair. You deserve to get the dreamy good guy."

My eyes welled up, and I swallowed the lump that had suddenly formed in my throat. I blinked the tears away. Apparently vampires could develop tears and ergo cry. Great.

I shared how I was hoping Concetta could help me out. But that was all the catching up she had time for. She had barely chewed as she ate and was now clearing the table so she could rush back to her desk.

I was driving to my basement apartment to unload the boxes there, but I remembered the will was to be read and I had just enough time to get back to the Amherst mansion. I would have to figure out where to keep the files after the reading of the will.

I went directly to the study, where Ainsley said they would meet. I slipped in, closing the door softly, and stood in a corner. The room had real wood paneling, paintings on the wall spot-lighted by track lighting, mood lighting from the Tiffany style floor lights scattered around. Their peacock design lamp shades gave a touch of whimsy to the otherwise somber room.

This was my idea of a cozy place to curl up and read, but I felt it was used more as a casual meeting room. It had a mix of pretension with the tasteful artwork to impress and yet the chairs were in a circle for conversation.

They hadn't begun yet. They all sat in leather chairs: Ainsley, Finley and his son Graham, and the betrayed college friend-Brooklyn. The lawyer, a middle-aged man, had a thick middle and bags under his eyes, yet his barely graying hair had an expensive cut and he had a status sports watch. He was just arranging his papers on his lap. They could've met in a room with a table or desk at least to make this easier.

The lawyer looked at his watch and I realized we were waiting for others to join. We didn't have to wait long. The door quietly opened and the three employees entered: the helpful maid Kathlyn Parker, chef Caleb Naylor, who I'd met just yesterday, and the gardener, Ethan Spencer. Ethan took a moment to give me a wink and a sly smile.

Ethan's scuffed and muddy work boots, standard denim pants with some grass stains, and standard polo shirt seemed out of place and conspicuous. He swiped a baseball cap off his head as he glanced around. His eyes had crow's feet, and the crevices were evident.

I could hear their hearts beating a bit faster than usual. The staff's hearts were faster, perhaps anxious, while the guests were calm. I imagine it was unusual for staff who hadn't been employed here long to be in the will.

The lawyer cleared his throat and began. The house, grounds, and vacation homes and everything within went to Ainsley. The business was Ainsley's with the proviso that Finley was the second in command, and he would mentor Ainsley and assist her. Finley would receive pay and bonuses commensurate with his position. Ainsley would receive all of Victoria's power to take the company into the future.

Ainsley's head lowered into her hands. She didn't seem to take the news well.

"The business should always be in the Amherst family's hands, but my sister never learned the business. She must now step up and take over the family's interests and legacy. Finley was always good with the business aspects, and I'm

asking that he put aside any disappointment and work with Ainsley."

Finley's face was scarlet while his hands on the chair arms were white knuckled. Finley's son, Graham, was provided with a trust that seemed generous, considering he was a teen when Victoria and Finley married. Graham let out a few expletives, expressing his opinion on what he should have received, and stormed out, slamming the door.

CHAPTER ELEVEN

The three staff members jumped when the door slammed. Ethan and Kathlyn glanced at each other while Caleb looked directly ahead as if he was in boot camp. They didn't have to wait long. The lawyer explained they would each get small gifts of a few thousand and if Ainsley didn't keep them employed as her staff, they would get letters of recommendation.

All three looked to Ainsley, their eyes filled with a question.

Ainsley raised her head from her hands and looked at them. "Please stay on while I figure out what I'm going to do with everything."

There were a few other gifts bestowed, but Brooklyn was the last.

"To Brooklyn I bequeath the house in Malibu as my apology for ever getting involved with her fiance. I never told anyone, but he cheated on me within a month. We both deserved better, and I shouldn't have let him come between us."

Brooklyn's eyebrows reached for the sky in surprise. I couldn't tell if it was the news of getting a Malibu house or the serial cheating of her ex-fiance.

Finley marched out the door and the others filed out, but I stayed while Ainsley sat in her chair. Her heartbeat was rapid and she seemed in distress.

The estate lawyer tapped his stack against his lap to align them. "Ainsley, I'll inform the corporation of the will and that you are now the head of the company. But I strongly urge you to either fly to the headquarters first thing or, at the very least, arrange a zoom meeting with the executives to begin your transition into the leadership role."

She wrung her hands, then ran them through her hair. "I don't know what to do. I'm not meant for this and I don't want it."

The lawyer secured all his paperwork in his brief-case and stood. "You'll have to figure it out. Hundreds of people are now your responsibility." He looked at me and shrugged, then walked out the door. His job was done.

I took pity on her and walked to her. "I can help you to your room." I took her elbow and led her into the hallway. She shrugged off my hand. "Thank you, but I can find my way. I appreciate your concern." She wiped the tears from her face, squared her shoulders, and walked away.

"You need to be extra cautious. The news that you have inherited the business and fortune will make at least local and business news. The killer may very well come after you as well."

She had stopped and faced me, but didn't answer. No doubt, she was overwhelmed by all that had been placed in her lap.

"All I'm asking is to not take any risks and let me know if you plan any activity that could leave you exposed. I can help."

She nodded, then turned and walked away. I followed at a distance. I followed until she went into her room.

· · ·

I retreated to my room. I wished the Amhersts had video surveillance in the hallways so I could monitor who came and went. Of course, that would have shown who had set the fire and we would be far closer to solving who killed Victoria.

My cell phone was vibrating in my pocket. Concetta was finally calling after my two voicemails I'd left her earlier in the day.

I answered with more desperation in my voice than I planned. "I'm so glad you called me back."

"What is going on? I don't hear from you outside our mentoring sessions. The last one was only two nights ago, and now I'm getting two voicemails in a day. What in the world does Leif want to talk about?"

I took a few deep breaths before answering. "He said something about my not dating one of the vampires he introduced me to a few weeks ago."

"Oh. Oh, no," was her only reply.

My voice went up an octave. "What does that mean? What aren't you telling me?"

"Leif wants all vampires in relationships. I'd hoped with you being so newly turned that he would give you some adjustment time, but with you working with a witch…"

My heart plummeted to my shoes. All positivity seemed to drain away, and I was left with deep sorrow. I never wanted to be a vampire, and this rogue destroyed the life I was just building for myself. My eyes filled with tears waiting to fall.

"This is unacceptable. I won't have him dictating my life to me." I intended to sound adamant and fierce, but it came out as discouraged and a little desperate. I let out a sob as the tears started flowing. I could definitely cry as a vampire.

"Oh, don't cry dear. Look, I'll go with you and try to talk to Leif, try to buy you some more time."

"What good will that do? It's just delaying it. He'll

still try to run my life." I sniffed and dabbed my eyes dry.

"What you need is a beard. A male vampire who wants his freedom, who'll pretend to be your significant other. I think I have just the right vampire in mind, too."

I hesitated. This was getting too complicated with Rowen and our trying to be friends on the sly and get to know each other behind everyone's back. Adding a fake relationship seemed another layer of deception that would increase the odds of messing up. But, looking for the silver lining, this could work and get Leif to leave me alone. I must've been quiet too long.

"Unless you're already thinking of a relationship with that witch?" Suspicion oozed through her voice.

Concetta may have been a wild child in the nineteen-sixties, but I don't know how she felt about the forbidden topic of vampires mixing with other Meta species. I couldn't risk it.

"How would... I mean, how does this work, this fake dating?" I closed my eyes and silently swore. I had to explain this all to Rowen and hope he understood and didn't just give up on the entire idea of us, whatever that might look like. That would be very awkward looking for the rogue vampire together if we were barely speaking. Besides the knife through my heart.

"I know a vampire that's a wild one, and he doesn't want to settle down. He and Leif have had their *meetings* over the decades. He is a Don Juan type–the love them and leave them fun-time guy. If he agrees to be seen with you around vampires as if you're dating and seen going in and out of each other's apartments, you can then do your own things without Leif troubling you."

Wow, a morally loose vampire didn't sound promising. It sounded so dangerous and I was sure if Leif discovered what we were doing, even Concetta would feel his wrath. I chewed on a thumbnail.

"Oh, I guess it's better than being forced into a relationship that nobody really wants. That's a recipe for really long-term hell. How do we sell this to Leif?"

She would make a phone call to the vampire she had in mind and see if he was willing to deceive the head of the vampires in Majestic so he could have his exploits. I had a few hours before I had to be at Leif's house, in which time I still had things to do. But I ended up pacing in my room feeling overwhelmed.

The rogue vampire, Victoria's murder, trying to keep My Private Sherlock operating while my boss attempted to salvage his marriage and hide the fact I wasn't a licensed investigator while adjusting to being a vampire, and sneaking around to see Rowen in stolen moments, and now adding a fake relationship was overwhelming to say the least.

You'd think being practically immortal would have its perks, but I hadn't seen one yet.

A knock on my door pulled me out of my never ending swirl of thoughts. It was Rowen. I just knew it. I opened the door and there he was, smiling at me and his eyes twinkling. I let out a shaky breath.

"What happened, Misty? Are you all right?" He stepped into the bedroom and closed the door.

I started pacing back and forth again. "Leif wants to meet with me. He terrifies me, so I called Concetta."

He let me pace and talk in my own way and time. He sat on the bed, watching me go back and forth without saying a word. When I finished telling about Concetta's looking for a fake vampire boyfriend, he ran his hands through his hair.

"It all happened so fast. I didn't know what else to do. When I hesitated at her suggestion of a fake boyfriend, she asked if it was because of you? That terrified me, because I didn't think she would understand, no matter how sympathetic she tries to be."

He stared at me, his eyes a mix of emotion. "That explains why Rebecca, the head of the witches and council representative, asked to meet with me. I think they're concerned about us working together. They are stepping in on both of us." He stood and took my hand. "We can give in and once the rogue vampire is caught, keep our distance from one another... or we can find a way to work around the obstacles and continue to be friends... and get to know each other. Either way won't be easy, but one is safer." He looked in my eyes as he said it, looking for my answer.

So he was being pressured as well, and the Council suspected something was up between us. I don't know how. We rarely got much time together, and working at Amherst was supposed to be away from their eyes.

"I think we made a mistake thinking we could be ourselves here. I don't think any place is really safe from their monitoring." I had to be clear about how I felt with him. "But if you're asking me how I want to proceed, I'd like to keep, you know, being friends. If there's a way to make it work, I want to try. I don't have many close friends and I don't like being told who I can turn to through life's challenges. You've been a good friend and I don't want to lose that or what this can become."

He nodded. "Okay then, we each start a fake relationship. I'll think of more enchanted ways for us to communicate and spend time together. We'll work around these obstacles. But promise me if it becomes too much for either of us or if one of us no longer wishes to go through with this, we tell the other and we let it go." I nodded.

I didn't even want to think of such an ending, but it was only fair. We didn't know what we were facing or how hard this would be.

"I really want to kiss you, but I don't know if Leif or other vampires could tell." He raised my hand and kissed it. It was so romantic and gentlemanly, it made me warm all over. Surely a simple kiss to my hand wouldn't leave traces. He leaned his forehead against mine. "I'll try to find a way magically for us to have a safe place to meet. But until then we placate Leif and Rebecca and find the rogue while beginning our cover relationships."

It felt like we were spies from competing countries trying to hide not only our real identities, but risking so much to have time together. I couldn't believe the twist my life had taken in the last few months. I became a vampire, which was likely the worst event of my life, but yet it brought me to Rowen, one of the best things in my life.

My cell phone rang. Concetta. Rowen and I looked at each other, knowing this would tell if she had a cover for me or not.

* * *

I met Concetta at a bar in the lakeside lodge before going to Leif's meeting. She introduced me to Travis, the wanton Casanova vampire who would pretend to be my boyfriend. He reminded me of several high school boys who were popular with girls, but I didn't have a thing in common with and who routinely made my life hell back then.

We eyed each other until I offered my hand. "Thank you for agreeing to this arrangement. I know you have your reasons, but I'm still adjusting to this new life and I don't want to be pressured into dating to please somebody else." He shook my hand and visibly relaxed.

Travis wasn't good looking in the suave, stylish sense like Rowen, but he had that All American athlete look with blond hair, blue eyes, and a mischievous smile that promised a good time and no strings. He wasn't particularly tall, but he was muscular in his form fitting henley shirt. I'm sure many vampires– or not, and females–or not, found him irresistible. I wasn't one of them.

Concetta cut through the awkwardness. "There is no sense trying to say you two found each other or such nonsense. Leif will see through subterfuge. So we stick to the facts as much as possible. We just aren't forthcoming with the true motivation for the two of you." Which was that Travis would be far more discrete in his promiscuous ways while we outwardly *dated* and my life remained private and my own.

Even Concetta didn't want to cross Leif more than necessary. *Gulp.* I drove my own vehicle, but Concetta and Tristan took his truck. Leif's house was average and nothing special. It blended into the neighborhood. The one thing it had was a larger lot of land and a six-foot privacy fence around it. A half-circle driveway that allowed for many cars to park without bothering the neighbors.

The three of us approached the front door, but it opened abruptly. Leif greeted us by waving us to get in-side. Leif was more like Conan the Barbarian in jeans. He had strong Nordic ancestry with blond hair a little past his collar, blue eyes, muscles like chiseled rocks, and an aura that telegraphed he could and would kill without blinking. From my first meeting with him, I didn't trust him and suspected he was manipulative and controlling.

The interior of his house displayed his heritage proudly. He had paintings of vikings, old maps of Norway, and a double-headed ax on the living room walls and a bust of a fierce-looking viking on a coffee table. The furniture was traditional but comfortable looking in neutrals with plenty of blood red accents and leather everywhere. It was tastefully decorated and somehow wasn't a man cave. The many plants, including elephant ears, Aloe Vera, and hanging spider plants, gave the space balance and cozy feel.

Leif extended a massive hand to indicate we should sit. Travis and I sat next to each other on a loveseat to begin our charade and Concetta took an end of the couch. Leif stood, towering over us and shrinking the room by his presence. I recognized the intimidation tactic from my father and focused on getting through this with our plan successfully.

"I wasn't expecting anyone besides Miss Summers. Concetta, what is the meaning of this?" A bushy eyebrow rose as he glared at Concetta.

Concetta appeared cool, but I suspected she had a healthy awareness of how dangerous Leif truly was and how to work this out with him.

"You terrified our Misty, and so she turned to me. Sometimes it takes a softer touch to accomplish what you aggressively push." She nodded towards us on the loveseat. "Travis has been on the receiving end of your demands to stop tom-catting around and it has only caused hard feelings." Travis looked at a map on the wall while he clenched his jaw.

"As for Misty, frankly, she has gone beyond any other newbie in trying to track that rogue vampire." Travis glanced at me with surprise in his eyes. Concetta held up her hand to stop Leif countering her. "I know you made it a condition of allowing her to keep the job she loves. Still, you ask a lot and now you are controlling her personal life too. Within a matter of weeks, her entire world has been tossed upside down, and she has a demanding task master commandeering her life."

He turned his dark look on me and I forced myself to gaze directly into his eyes, not in challenge, but to show it was all true. I tried to look a bit sad as well. I willed him to understand, to have some compassion.

He looked between Travis and me. "Are you trying

to tell me they have somehow met and Travis is so smitten he'll stop his cavorting and I won't have to concern myself any longer with her becoming too close with a witch?" He scoffed. Travis glanced my way and raised an eyebrow.

So Rowen was what brought this all about, as I had suspected. The way he worded it told me he didn't know anything for certain, but he clearly suspected we might get closer. That wasn't good, and I was glad Rowen and I were taking steps already to keep our close relationship even more secret.

Should we stop before our hearts are too invested in each other? Because we seem doomed before we even get started and we could get into a lot of trouble. I didn't even know what the punishment would be and hadn't wanted to know before.

Concetta answered Leif's question. "No, we all know how unlikely that would be. But I have introduced Travis and Misty and suggested that they agree to an arrangement with a ninety-day trial in which they will date one another and give it an honest try. This allows them to both seek peace with you while it is still their choice. They have agreed to this solution."

The three of us held our breath and waited as Leif scrutinized Travis and I. This was even worse than being sent to a principal's office. His anger seemed barely contained and I swear I could see the air around him vibrate. I swallowed loudly and looked at the carpet.

CHAPTER TWELVE

"*T*ravis is the last vampire I would've considered for her, but perhaps she'll be good for him. I wanted a... more responsible companion to aid her through this adjustment period, not cause more upset in her life." He paused. Travis had stiffened next to me as Leif made no effort to spare his feelings. *How rude.*

I caught Concetta narrowing her eyes at Leif as if she saw through him.

"But if it has already been agreed to, I will allow it." He finally said.

Why was Concetta suspicious of Leif? Who did he have in mind for me? It was probably best I didn't know.

"I don't like this arrangement and I think it isn't advisable. It's highly likely we'll be having this conversation again in ninety days. Which would be a record for Travis, if he lasts that long." His gaze made clear his opinion of Travis, and I could see why they didn't get along.

I was struck by how neither Travis nor Concetta seemed upset that he would "allow" us to date. They just accepted Leif has the authority to make those decisions. I didn't think I would ever get used to that. But for the moment, we had a reprieve. I hoped Rowen's meeting with Rebekah was going as well. Phase one of our fake dating was in place. It all had happened so fast, but it was better than Leif dictating my personal life, right?

Travis was more attentive as we left, placing his hand on my lower back and opening the front door and car door for me. I began to think Travis sought a string of hook-ups to compensate for something else lacking in his life, based on his reactions to Leif's low opinion of him. But it wasn't for me to pry. He would open up if he felt like it.

I certainly understood life's disappointments, my parents being a prime example. They were consumed with their own lives and my brother, who was their shining golden child. I vowed years ago not to let it get to me and I adopted the positive thinking philosophy and sought professional help.

We had agreed they would follow me to my apartment and he would help me unload all the boxes of Amherst employee files before he took Concetta home. This way he would know where my home was since we agreed to be seen at each other's places.

The entire drive over, I fretted over the fake dating scheme, worried what Leif would do if he found it was a smoke screen, a scam to keep him out of our lives.

It was dark when we parked on the street in front of my place. I opened up my doors and trunk and grabbed two boxes stacked. Travis grabbed two as well, and we walked to the house.

"You own a house?" Surprise was evident in his voice.

"No, I just rent the basement apartment. It works out great, though."

"Is that your door open, then?"

I looked and saw my door, in the sunken space under the stairs to the house, standing open and felt a wave of dread sweep over my body and choke my throat. I dropped my boxes and ran to the door.

Travis and Concetta stopped behind me and we saw my apartment had been ransacked. But worse was the note stuck to my door with a knife. *Quit looking for me, or you'll be sorry,* was all it said. Effective and to the point.

Fear hit my thoughts. "Winston!" and I ran inside.

"Who's Winston?" I heard Travis ask.

"Her adorable cat. I hope the little fur-ball is okay." Concetta answered him.

I ran to the bedroom and got on my hands and knees, calling my sweet kitty and looking under the bed. Concetta joined me and Travis stopped at the doorway. My room had been tossed but wasn't too bad.

Concetta laid a hand on my shoulder. "He's here. I can hear his heartbeat. He's still scared." I hadn't even focused for a heartbeat. I was so scared. She pointed to a corner of the top shelf in the closet.

Concetta turned to Travis. "Go into the kitchen and look for any canned cat food you can find. Open and dump it in a bowl and bring it."

I was speaking softly to Winston, telling him it was alright. Travis handed me Winston's special soft food in a dish, and I placed it on the shelf for him.

It's around time you came back to me. We had a predator break in—big and scary. I thought he would kill me, eat me even.

"Winston dear, don't be so melodramatic. He's gone and he won't hurt you." I didn't know that for sure, but he needed to feel safe again. "I'll put extra locks on buddy."

He finally took a paw and slid the dish of canned food closer and took a few delicate bites. *I can't let this food go to waste. Besides, I need to keep my strength up. That scared at least a few years off one of my nine lives.*

Travis was fascinated. "I've never known a vampire to have a pet."

"I had Winston when I was turned. He's adjusting through this, too." I turned to Winston. "Winston honey, this is Travis. He may be around a bit, but he won't hurt you at all. I promise." I gave Travis a side eye, and he nodded.

Winston looked Travis over. *I like Courtney better. I'll be watching him.*

I tried not to smile at his protective side, always looking out for me.

Concetta got on her cell phone. "Leif, the rogue vampire tossed Misty's place."

She hung up, but I knew he would be here in just a few minutes. This was the worst day after my date from hell when I was turned into a vampire. I didn't know if I would ever feel safe in my place again. I needed Rowen to do a spell for protection. I just needed Rowen right now, not everybody else around me. But I had to get through the next hour or so.

I grabbed Concetta's arm as fear gripped me again. I looked up, meaning my landlady, who lived in the rest of the house.

She whisked out of my room and shortly I heard Mrs. Macksimowitz, or Mrs M., chatting away with Concetta, saying she was no bother and Misty lived in the basement, just down under the stairs. I just wasn't at home right now, no bother at all. I released a loud breath of relief.

"I've never known a vampire so invested in a human, either." He eyed me like an odd specimen.

"I've known her most of my life, and she is a gentle soul. She renovated this basement with me in mind. I couldn't bear it if she were hurt because of me."

"Nobody I grew up with is alive anymore, so I understand. It's just been so long for me."

"When were you born?" I wasn't sure if that was the

proper way to ask, but it sounded better than asking when he died.

"1910." He shrugged his shoulders. "Leif keeps telling me I'm old enough to grow up and be responsible." That explained some of Leif's attitude. Travis certainly had been around awhile and likely seen a lot besides the moon landing, two world wars, the industrial and electronics revolution, as well as cars and planes. That should sober anybody, I would think, but it seemed he was the ultimate Peter Pan wanting to stay in the Casanova stage of many young males. Or perhaps facing immortality reinforced an *eat, drink, and be merry* sort of jaded attitude. I could see either side. I didn't agree with the latter.

"It's going to be hard for me when I lose the people I care about. But for now, I'm just relieved Winston and Mrs. M are okay."

"We've all been through it. We should have a support group, actually." He gave a lopsided smile. "What about your parents?"

"Oh, my parental units never showed me even a smidgen of affection or consideration. It's as if I don't have any parents." I don't even get emotional when I talk about it anymore. Okay, maybe a little bitterness remains.

He gave me a hug, not like Rowen's, where I feel his strength and caring soak into me, but a brief friendship hug from barely an acquaintance. *Awkward.*

Leif and Concetta walked in together as I was just getting Winston down and holding him close. Leif's overpowering presence spooked him and he jumped back onto the closet shelf and cowered in the corner with a yelp. I ushered everyone into the living room and closed my bedroom door so Winston could settle down.

"Why do you still have that cat? Vampires don't have

pets." This had been a long day with plenty of ups and downs, so his comment set me off.

"This is my home, Leif. You can leave now if you can't respect that." I folded my arms and glared at him. I had never spoken like that to anybody, ever. He really knew how to push my buttons and it didn't bode well for getting along with him long term. From the look in his eyes, I might not survive much longer to worry about it. Note to self: write your will, so Winston has a home to go to. Maybe Mrs. M or Courtney would take him.

Concetta stepped between us. "The issue isn't the cat, it is the rogue vampire. Let's stay focused."

"I think the issue is more about how he knew where I live." Then a thought struck me like a thunderbolt. "Actually…"

Travis had been watching me with shock after my reply to Leif and noticed. "What? What're you thinking?"

"Yes, what *are* you thinking?" Leif's murderous look had changed to business.

"At one time you said that a vampire who turns someone…"

Leif had to be in charge. "The sire."

"… the sire usually has some sort of connection to the sired vampire. Since I was a hit-and-run siring, you didn't think there would be a connection. But if there is, can he sense where I am and find me that way?"

Leif answered as if he were teaching a class, not discussing my life. "Of course it's possible. But every-thing we know about the bond informs us that, like any relationship, it needs time to develop and strengthen any bond. Yours was less than a one-night stand."

Concetta glared at him while Travis's mouth fell open.

"You really know how to make a girl feel special." I

snarled. He couldn't have been more crass and hurtful if he had set out to do so.

Leif's scowl intensified. "Let me stop you right now. We don't really know how the connection works. I can't break any bond you might have with your sire, and no I don't know how you can trace it back to him. There are many things we have yet to understand."

Concetta cleared her throat, and we all looked at her. "But we do know that the older the vampire, the more unusual adaptations occur. One vampire of seven hundred and fifty years dead eventually could hear his sire's thoughts. Rumor has it that one vampire of six hundred years dead could compel people like the movies have Dracula do. If this Jack Anderson is old enough, he could have a bond with no effort or time together necessary."

Another thought occurred to me. I looked at Leif. "This may be more about challenging you than threatening me."

"How do you possibly get that?" He crossed his arms like I was laying blame for everything on him.

"Let me work this through. The last time we had anything from Jack was when he turned and left that girl at Crossed Oars Tavern! You personally own the Tavern. It's been a few weeks since we last had anything happen from him. No sightings, no illegal turnings, no word. He's just dropped out of sight." I held up my finger to give me a minute while I paced. "I don't know how much the vampire community elsewhere knows about local Meta Mundane Council members, but it's possible he knew you were the Vampire grand poobah here. So what if that note is more to warn you and therefore the Council to back off because somebody under your authority or protection is now in danger? If he were able to find me because of some connection, no matter how slim, I could be the conduit to tell you to back off."

Leif stared at me for a minute, then slowly nodded his head. "That's actually feasible. I'm not just a local Vampire Representative, but I'm part of the higher District Council for three states. He could very well have heard who I am, even with minimal contact with a vampire community, and heard the Crossed Oars Tavern was mine." He shook his head. "I should've made that connection. But he has to know his reckless behavior will only make the Council view him as more of a threat and be more determined to stop him."

Oh great, he was a bigger deal than just the local vampire boss. He was the vampire boss overseeing three states. His ingrained prejudices were pushed in three states.

I shook my head. "I think he has actually made it clear he won't back down and is warning you. If he knew you lived nearby, maybe he could sense another powerful vampire in the vicinity. This could be like trespassing into your territory and saying you can't stop him."

I glanced at Concetta and Travis. She had her hands clasped against her mouth while Travis looked at me in surprise. Apparently, I was an oddity and continually unique for a vampire.

"I must gather the vampires. We must flush him out and end this."

Concetta beat me to raising an objection. "That seems exactly what he wants you to do. He has said he won't follow the Council's rules on turning vampires as he sees fit, which those laws are entirely to keep our presence from people and prevent vampire hunts like during the Crusades. If you have a vampire posse essentially hunting him down, the potential of mundane people to see and become fully aware of our presence is practically guaranteed."

I saw my opportunity and jumped in. "I also think it's a terrible idea. You have a Meta Council with many meta species, while he's a lone vampire as far as we know. Our strength is not Vampires, or spells from witches, but all tehr Meta's abilities used together that can stop Jack Anderson. I was there when the Meta Council voted a harsh judgment on him, so work together to bring him to justice. Truly, your strength is in being united and that can lower the risk of mundane people being alerted to our presence."

"I'll consider it, and I'll call a Council Meeting and discuss our response with them."

CHAPTER THIRTEEN

*L*eif left shortly. With Concetta and Travis helping me at vampire speed, most everything was cleaned up and back to normal in an hour. While cleaning up, I had the chance to ask about something she had said.

"What did you mean about the vampire hunts of the Crusades earlier?"

Travis grimaced. "I'm leaving that for Concetta to explain. That's too grim for me." Which was startling as stories of battles and war seemed most men's favorite. "I'm a lover, not a fighter." He chuckled.

Concetta took a deep breath. "It isn't pleasant, but it is our history…" She gave an abbreviated explanation of the Crusades, typically known as the period when the Catholic Church waged war over perceived holy sites of both Muslim and Christian beliefs but surprisingly also was the cover of an actual genocide of vampires on a staggering and horrific scale.

She shared with such insight that I suspected she had once been a teacher, or even a governess, depending upon how old she really was. I didn't think she was old enough to have lived through the events, but I wouldn't bet on that. Someday I would ask her about her background, but not tonight.

The employment records from Amherst Mattress were all unloaded and dumped around my small dining area for me to delve into shortly. Concetta and Travis were about to leave when a knock on the door made me stiffen and look at each of them. I swallowed and approached the door slowly.

Surprise didn't cover the feelings that assaulted me to see Rowen standing at the door with Rebekah, the witch representative on the Council, and another woman with him. The blank look in Rowen's eyes and his clenched jaw told me to keep everything formal. Although, he looked me over as if to make sure I was unharmed. My gaze took in the other young woman, who I guessed was his fake date candidate. She was the opposite of me, dark straight hair, dark eyes, mysterious, and the very image of a witch with flowing black clothes.

I felt deflated. She was amazing with a presence that hit you immediately. I hadn't felt so inconsequential since high school. I straightened my spine and commanded myself to project confidence. I wasn't in high school anymore, and Rowen and I were going to great lengths to develop a relationship of some sort. He wouldn't go through this trouble if he were going to dump me at the first seductive witch he crossed. Besides, he likely already knew her in order to so quickly have her as a candidate to pretend to be his girlfriend.

Rebekah spoke for them. "Leif called and said you had a visit from the rogue vampire and needed some magical protection."

Concetta stepped in and took over. "Rebekah, thank you for coming over so quickly. Please come in. Travis and I have helped Misty cleanup the damage so you have perfect timing."

The threesome walked in and began sprinkling salt at the doors and windows while chanting, then walked clockwise through the entire basement, including my bedroom and bathroom while flinging some sort of water from finger bowls around, also chanting the entire time. I could feel invisible walls go up, the energy vibrating and pulsating.

I tried not to follow them with my eyes, watching Rowen with the young woman, but it was hard. He didn't give any hint we were close. The young witch was graceful and like smoke drifting and floating. She probably never tripped over her own feet like I did. But wouldn't ephemeral perfection get boring?

I looked away and caught Travis staring at me. He flickered a glance at Rowen and quirked an eyebrow up. I was being too obvious, and that wasn't good. I also couldn't help but compare myself to the lovely witch that seemed a perfect fit for Rowen. They both had that dark intensity.

I wondered about the wisdom of this entire plan when it conspired for Rowen to be in the orbit of that dark-haired version of Stevie Nicks. I reminded myself this was all to give us a chance at something. Maybe it would only ever be friendship. I shouldn't get so invested, but just let things unfold.

It took all of twenty minutes for Rowen and the two ladies to be done and leave. Rowen darted a look behind his shoulder on the way out. I knew he would contact me through the locket when it was safe.

I took a deep breath and attempted a look that wasn't confused but rather self assured despite my place being violated and seeing Rowen with a stone-cold gorgeous witch.

After the three witches were gone and I checked through the apartment for anything else to clean up , Travis spoke to Concetta. She left to wait for Travis at his truck. She studied both of us for a minute before giving me a hug goodnight and leaving.

Travis approached me slowly, as if I was going to

run. "I thought Leif was exaggerating." He paused and started over. "I have a talent for feeling people's vibes, emotions, since before I was a vampire. Being a vampire made it even more heightened. The good news is that I'm the only vampire I know of with this ability, but Leif has guessed something's up between you two. That witch, Rebekah, doesn't trust you at all. Maybe only because you're a vampire and working with the handsome witch. But I sensed she is interested in him for herself."

I covered my face with my hands. No need to try to hide it if he sensed it. I managed not to cry, although my eyes were filled, and I blinked to keep the tears from spilling out. My life had become a soap opera version of an old Munsters show. It would be laughable if it weren't my reality.

"That other witch has absolutely no interest in your guy, none, zip. None for me, either. So he picked well if they're playing the same game we are. That's really what you're doing, isn't it? A smokescreen for the Council to leave you two alone, right?"

If he could see through it, how long would it take Leif and Rebekah? Oh, this was doomed, even though the news of the young sultry witch not showing any interest in Rowen was encouraging. Still, it felt like my entire life had become a soap opera, perhaps Dark Shadows Redux.

"You can't tell anyone, ever. I don't want to find out what'll happen if the Council finds out. It shouldn't be any of their business. It's the freaking twenty-first century." I huffed.

"I agree with you, but the meta community tends to hold old traditions closely and is even slower to change than feuding Capulets and Montagues. I'm relieved I don't have to worry about you getting interested in me while we play this charade. I'm willing to help you two out and play along. So, what else do we do to sell this dating thing?"

I was glad to have somebody helping with this, but I was also leery of his quick acceptance of Rowen and I and willingness to aid and abet our violating the laws.

"Um, sensing some fear to trust me, okay. That's probably for the best."

"I don't know how vampires date, so what would you do for a date?"

He coughed and rubbed a hand across the back of his neck. "I tend to meet a young human at a bar or something… I rarely see them again after the night. I'm not into second dates, so this is new for me."

"Okay, fair enough. Wait. You can mingle with humans, but I can't be friends with a witch?" He would have plenty of tourists to go through with a fresh supply regularly.

"Oh please, when Rowen looks at you, it isn't like a friend. That wizard has it bad for you, and I believe you are just as head-over-heels for him."

I got back to the original point. "Since we don't have to worry about either of us falling for the other, should we go to live music or something?" Dinner was out for the moment, so that left movies, museums, and music.

He smiled and the All-American athlete look became pure charisma that promised a broken heart. I had to send a thanks to the universe that I never found that playboy charm attractive. "That's a good idea. I expect Leif will have eyes on us, so word will get back to him. But can it be in a couple of days?"

"I have to keep working on the case out at the Amherst mansion, so a few days will help me out." I wanted to wrap that up. Besides, now the problem with the rogue vampire was reaching critical mass.

Travis had his hand on the front doorknob when he turned. "I wouldn't risk seeing your McDreamy witch for a while, okay?" He winked and was out the door. He had charm to spare, but I was still unsure how much to trust him.

I stood, looking at my place, and found I was angry at Jack Anderson for violating my space and upsetting my darling Winston. I found my adorable tuxedo cat on my bed, curled in a tight ball. I picked him up and held him close while I started unpacking some files. He stayed in my arms or lap as I worked separating out the files of employees who were laid off because of the closure. The files had employees from prior years mixed throughout. I focused and poured on the vampire speed.

Within an hour and a half, I had gone through every box and had rough piles set up. Winston had finally calmed down and went to sleep in my arm hanging partially over my shoulder. I had found several files that contained newspaper clippings of any mention of Amherst Mattress in the local news. Ah yes, before print news was replaced by fleeting online write-ups..

I grabbed those news pieces and began skimming, looking for employees quoted who were angry over the layoff. The third folder contained multiple articles on the plant closure and I began taking notes of any names.

The most helpful were the "letters to the editor" regarding the closure. While the majority were justifiably scared for the town's future, there were several who called out the wealthy Amherst family, but only a few letters were seething about Victoria Amherst's cavalier disregard for the entire town's well-being while she "sipped champagne and shopped at Oscar De LaRenta and Louis Vuitton." I noted their names and placed an asterisk next to them as definitely potential threat writers.

I found the files of the people I had written down and got ready to go back to the Amherst mansion. I decided I couldn't leave Winston after the scare he'd had, so I backed up his litter pan and food dishes into the car and finally got him in a carrier.

The enchanted cameo locket vibrated under my collar, where it was pinned before I opened the door. Rowen was calling through our secret communications jewelry. I opened the locket and tried to look nonchalant.

I was nervous and jumped in. "How did your meeting go?" I kicked myself for not at least saying hello first.

His face seemed tired, especially around the eyes. "Not as well as I'd hoped. Rebekah argued with us a good bit, not believing that we'd started dating. Simone is more into Tina Marie than me, and Rebekah had suspected it. Simone was already fearing some extreme measures, so she jumped at a deal with me." That explained why *Simone* wasn't interested in Rowen even a little. What a perfect name for the dark and alluring witch I'd seen.

What he didn't mention was the risk if it were found out we conspired to deceive the Council.

I plopped down on my couch. "Am I safe talking here? I mean, could Rebekah have magically bugged my place while doing the protection spells?" Yeah, I didn't trust her.

"I thought about that and purposely did a final round to do an anti-listening spell. I didn't have a lot of time to come up with something and I'll probably need to slip in later and do a better version, but it should do the trick for now. Anybody listening in will hear you talking to Winston a lot."

Rowen ran a hand through his hair and let out a sigh. I didn't know what to say. This was scary and frustrating and maddening all rolled up.

"Misty, we'll get through this. One day at a time." He tilted his head looking, through the locket. "Please tell me what you're feeling."

My heart squeezed. I'd never had anybody other than my Courtney consider what I was feeling.

"I'm scared and worried." I took a deep breath. "Are you sure you want to go through all this when you could just date another witch and not be a secret agent to have a relationship?" There I'd said it. Do you really want to go through this for *me*?

"Yes, I'm sure. We haven't gotten to progress like normal people and have pleasant dates or strolls along the lake, but I know I want to build what we have because I think we've got something that can be special. I'm willing to play secret agent man if we get the chance to determine for ourselves what we want. I'm working on a way for us to make up for the loss of dating in the traditional sense, but it's a complex spell, so give me some time."

I debated about sharing that Travis felt Rebekah was interested in him for herself, but decided that was just too much at this moment. We needed to keep from being overwhelmed by everything swirling around us. We agreed to a few days without seeing each other, not even to help on the Amherst case.

CHAPTER FOURTEEN

*W*e were both tired and said goodnight. I made the drive around the lake to the Amherst mansion on auto pilot. The last few days were taking their toll on me. My emotions were swirling all over and seemed overwhelming.

I was angry at Leif and the Meta establishment for their archaic ideas. My heart ached that this could be the end of a budding relationship with a good guy, and I was furious at the rogue, Jack Anderson. I had a lot of anger to unleash on him when I eventually cornered that rat. He had turned my life upside down.

My positive side was taking a beating.

I parked and made it through the bedroom window, first with Winston in his carrier and then lugging his accoutrements by half past midnight. I had the files stuffed in my purse. I looked around and nothing had been touched. It felt like I'd been gone for days rather than roughly sixteen hours.

Winston sniffed around. *Not much, considering how fancy the place is from the outside.*

"This is just a servant's room, not a luxury guest room. From what I've read, this is a nicer servant's place than most from back in the day. You'll be safe here and I'll be back soon. I've got to check the place out."

I walked the halls of the quiet house on power-walk speed. I encountered the lady ghost floating down a hallway. Seeing the lady ghost had me wondering. I was pretty sure she was Helene, the wife that Jedediah Amherst was suspected of killing? Her dance partner would have to be the gardener Helene was rumored to have fallen in love with. That was only logical. He certainly dressed like a working-class person of the era, not like the privileged class. Did that mean that Jedediah had not only murdered his wife, but also her lover? I needed to look into Helene more at some point.

I walked the guest wing where everybody seemed tucked in for the night except for one couple with loud passionate noises at their door. I could hear a heartbeat in the main part of the house and went in search of it. I found a man in the kitchen, his arms loaded with items from the refrigerator. I watched for a few moments as the man was about to make a large midnight snack. He was average height, dark hair, and olive complexion, suggesting perhaps Italian or Spanish heritage.

I cleared my throat and the refrigerator raider jumped and placed a hand over his heart.

"You gave me quite a start." His voice was rough, gravelly.

"I was just doing a final check for the night. Are you Austin Chesley?" His voice was like what I'd heard during the bugging last night.

He turned back to his sandwich preparation, piling a few more slices of deli ham onto the mountain forming on top of a bread slice. "That's me. You're the private investigator that Finley is so mad to have here."

"How did you know Victoria?" I needed to find out more about him, and this seemed a natural question.

"My wife, Sophie, was Victoria's sorority sister." He grabbed a knife and a Compari tomato to slice.

"Did you know Victoria well? Spend much time here over the years?" I leaned against the kitchen entryway.

"I've been to these soirees of Victoria's maybe two other times. I work for a non-profit and don't get a lot of vacation time. Usually, I'd rather go someplace other than with a bunch of snobs."

"But aren't you and your wife from the same social class?" It escaped my mouth before I thought better.

"Sophie is from money, but I'm not. I'm the dose of reality in her world. I was raised by a single mother and went to college on scholarships and grants. I work at a non-profit providing legal counsel to the disadvantaged in Los Angeles, where we live. Sophie is a lawyer at a big firm and brings in the big money. It works for us so long as we don't end up on opposing sides." He spread mayonnaise and added some lettuce, then placed the top slice of bread.

Nothing incriminating in that. It explained why he would take exception to Victoria's calloused closing of the Amherst facility. He probably saw scores of people who slid into poverty after losing a job. But was he a crusader who could have snapped over Victoria? Not likely years after the closure, unless there was more of a connection.

"Where did you grow up? I'm a native in town, and I don't think you're from around here."

"I grew up in the Seattle area, Tri-Cities. I went to UCLA law school, and that's where I met Sophie." He removed a bottle of wine from the wine fridge and grabbed a glass from the cupboard.

It was time to get to the heart of the matter. "I understand that you have some opinions about Ms. Amherst's closure of the facility here in town and how it hurt the economy."

"Yes, I do. I'm more vocal around this group because it may be the only time they get to hear how more profit for some can mean devastation to others living paycheck-to-paycheck. They have plenty. Victoria and her stockholders had plenty, but it was never enough. So she destroyed an entire town's economy to line pockets." He poured a dark red wine and sipped it. This late at night, in the subdued light, it looked like blood. "I may be the only person to proclaim that message to them. My hope is it makes them uncomfortable enough that they think about the human toll when they're making business decisions."

I pondered his words. If Victoria was killed because of her closing the plant, perhaps that would make even more of an impression on other CEOs. But so far, I didn't think this non-profit legal eagle would jeopardize everything for a demonstration. It's hard to say, though.

I could say he was the most interesting of the guests, hands down. He was real when most of them had a fake or superficial air. He knew what struggle was, he saw it every day, and he had a heart for the down-on-their luck. No, my instinct kept screaming it was somebody with a personal dispute with Victoria, not an ethical or moral one.

"Did you see any of the guests acting suspicious? Anybody you suspect of killing Victoria?" I watched him closely for any reaction.

He shook his head. "No ma'am. They all act strange to me. I'd rather talk about sports scores than stock exchange tips and I sure don't like flirting with married women like this lot seems to do. I haven't the vaguest idea who would kill Victoria Amherst."

I returned to my room and sat on the bed with a sigh. Winston curled up with me, unusually quiet. I was relieved I brought him with me, I would've worried about him after the breakin. I recited the affirmations I turned to when things were bleak, when my family's lack of affection got me down.

I am a valuable human being.

I value myself as a person.

I deserve happiness and joy.

I embrace my happiness.

I am strong and resilient.

I have made it through other challenges, and I will make it through this one.

I am enough and don't have to prove anything to anyone else.

It is OK to feel sad today because tomorrow is a fresh start.

I repeated them ten times each. I needed to focus on them in the next days.

I decided I'd go over the few employee files I'd brought with me. I thrust thoughts of Rowen and our situation aside, as well as thoughts of Helene and her gardener aside for now. I had work to do.

I went through the employee files, scouring the details. I gave particular attention to the writers of "letters to the editor" that were aimed at Victoria. Primarily, two employees sent letters, one that worked in the manufacturing of the mattresses and the other worked for the facilities department maintaining the buildings and grounds. She didn't recognize their names. It was too much to hope that the files might have photos of the employees used for any entry or access badges.

They didn't have photos and the best information in the individual employee files was the performance reviews of the persons of interest I had noted overall. From the twelve files I had brought with me, all of them were evaluated as great employees before the plant closure was announced, but nine of them had significant changes in attitude after they found out their jobs were being outsourced overseas by Victoria. Which coincided with the newspaper letters or interviews I had flagged.

I eventually took a few hours for regenerative

zoning out. Which was easier said than done when my mind continued to go over Rowen, Simone, Rebekah, Leif, Travis, Winston, and oh yeah, the rogue-Jack Anderson. That wasn't even to mention the puzzle of who killed Victoria. I didn't see any glaring signs of who killed her, but there had to be some clue or tidbit I was missing. I should ask Rowen to create a spell that would trigger a neon sign over the guilty person's head flashing "Killer." No doubt magic didn't work that way.

Morning arrived with a dry but overcast sunrise. I got little rejuvenation during my downtime and the sunrise made me even more sluggish. I dragged myself up and through my morning routine. I repeated my affirmations from last night again and fed Winston some soft food and gave him kisses he shrugged off, but seemed to love anyway.

I was really feeling the desire to be in the dark and rest until the sun went down. Was my body changing even more and I would need to be a night investigator, or was I just running on empty and needed some self-care and pampering? Maybe I should've had some liquid nourishment while at home last night. At the time, I didn't think it was necessary.

I was also at a dead end at the moment. I could turn over the names of old employees to the police, but then I would be waiting for them to find anything. I wanted to make some headway before guests left and I needed to feel like I was contributing to the investigation.

First, I called Detective Shields and gave him the twelve employee names and what details I could. He was surprised I had found that much.

"This is helpful. We'll do background on them."

"I keep thinking something must have changed recently to seek revenge after so many years."

"Yes, a trigger of some sort. I'll keep an eye out for such a stressor. Also, we have a bit more from the fire department. The brand of cigarette that started the fire that was the distraction was Morley or Llama. Have you found those anywhere, by chance?"

"No, I haven't." But I think it is time I search some homes and guest rooms. "Do you have home addresses for the three employees?"

"We don't have enough for a search warrant and don't go sneaking around illegally entering any homes. Any evidence obtained that way could be disqualified."

I let that drop and changed the subject. "What about that video posted online? Anything from that? Anything I should look for that can identify the killer?"

Detective Shields sighed in a long exhale. "Nothing on the video. It was loaded at an internet cafe in Ponderosa-Vale. Your efforts have helped, truly. I contacted the Portland office of the FBI for a profile of the killer. I finally heard back this morning with an emailed basic profile. Male, forty to fifty, methodical and intelligent, patient. You've already picked up on the fact that something must have happened recently to propel the person to exact revenge now."

"Well, I'm in a house with around ten men that fit that physical description. I'm focusing on the three staff members and ex-husband Finley, college rival Brooklyn, and the one guest named Austin I mentioned, unless you have something more for me to pursue?"

"Nothing to pursue, but regarding the arrival times of the guests. They all did indeed fly in on the day of the murder, but they could have arranged for someone locally to deliver the threatening notes."

He hesitated before adding, "One last thing. I tried to follow up on the idea of Helene Amherst's death and find any descendants from that family. They became pretty dispersed over the intervening years. I have a phone number for you. It's a lady from Helene's sister's progeny who is expecting your call. I felt it was better for you to follow that thread yourself." I noted the number on a slip of paper.

"I also followed your thoughts with the other side of the family. Perhaps the gardener may have never forgiven Jedediah and somebody in that family was enacting decades old revenge. Here is a living relation for Franklin Merton." I wrote that man's contact number too.

I was getting very frustrated with how slow and plodding this investigation was going. I wanted to go home with Winston and deal with my life right now. I couldn't wait any longer. It was time I started driving this bus rather than chasing behind. I hung up with the detective, knowing I'd be crossing boundaries shortly.

I dug a mouse toy out of my purse I had tucked away and tossed it for Winston to play with while I worked.

I called the phone number the Detective provided without much of an idea what to expect.

An elderly but pleasing woman's voice answered, and I introduced myself mentioning Detective Shields had spoken to her.

Her creaky voice picked up. "Oh, yes dear. The detective mentioned you had some questions. I'm Harlow Morgan. I'll try to answer your questions about my great, great aunt Helene."

So far, so good. "Can you tell me how the family felt about Jedediah Amherst?" I wanted to start slow.

"From what the talk was when I was a child listening in on conversations, Helene's father had arranged the marriage, thinking him an ambitious go-getter. Although, I picked up that Helene's mother wasn't for the match, but her concerns weren't given much weight." She shuffled around like she was propped up in bed.

"How did the family take the news of Jedediah

killing her?" The opening move towards finding out if somebody in the family might have exacted revenge.

"Well, I don't know specifically, but I always got the impression her father was rather indifferent, but she had a brother who was reportedly bitter about it and her mother was devastated."

"Would there be anybody alive today that might still hold a grudge against the Amherst family?" I was going out on a limb now and I hoped she wouldn't take offense.

"Oh, I see. Trouble for the Amhersts, I gather. Let me consider…" She was quiet for several seconds before continuing. "I can't see it. From what I've witnessed at the family reunions that include most of our dispersed family, too many are immersed in the latest technology, jobs, and dealing with life. The youngest ones have been even more distracted and don't seem interested in the travails of our lineage, let alone know anything about Helene."

I didn't seem to be getting anywhere, so it was time to bring up the really touchy subject. "I came across a local newspaper article that mentioned Helene was gone on travel for a few months in the last year before her murder. They hinted that she may have been avoiding a scandal and I know she was involved with an employee here. Do you know anything about that?" I crossed my fingers, literally.

"Mmmm. Yes. There were whispers about her and a lover. My grandmother told me once to be careful with a young man I was fond of or I would end up like Helene and be giving away a child to avoid ruin. She never mentioned it again, but I felt so sorry for Helene that it stayed with me. Now that I think about it, I believe she gave the child up because Jedediah wouldn't raise it, or perhaps would harm it."

It was terribly sad. But I remembered the look of absolute devotion between the two ghosts dancing. I was positive in my heart they were Helene and Franklin and she had given up their child to keep it safely away from Jedediah.

"Did your family ever look for the child, or perhaps that child's descendants made inquiries at some point?" I kept thinking there was something to be found from the past impacting today.

"I never heard of such a thing. But if somebody came around, most likely one of the men would've dealt with anyone asking questions along those lines. I've no doubt they wouldn't admit to such impropriety in our family." Her voice held some heat, and she didn't sound happy.

"I really appreciate your taking the time to answer my questions."

"I've enjoyed it. I always loved any stories about poor mistreated Helene and how she found, at least in some small measure, love in her life. As I said, most of the family now isn't interested in old moldy stories of our family's past, even the scandals."

"Just one more question. Was there anybody such as extended family or close friends to Helene who might have raised a child?"

"Helene had a very close friend from childhood who married. My grandmother also would point to this friend as a paragon of virtue and point out that she was blessed with a child after it seemed she was barren for several years. But now I have to wonder if they hadn't been willing to take in Helene's child and raise it as their own."

"By any chance, do you know the name of that family?"

"Oh, now you're really testing me." She chuckled. "My memory isn't that good, if I ever knew the names in the first place."

I got her home address just in case I found anything of Helene's to send to her. I think she'd like that. The conversation left me thinking Helene's dear friend raised the child. But what if a grandchild was making sure the grandkids of Jedediah Amherst paid for his treatment of Helene? It could happen. The letters could just be a smokescreen.

I made a call to Franklin Merton's living relative while I was on these threads from the past.

CHAPTER FIFTEEN

A youthful voice answered the call. I explained my search involving his ancestor, Franklin Merton.

"Yes, the Detective told me this was part of an on-going investigation and to expect your call. My name is Tyler, Tyler Merton. I'm the only one in my family who is into our genealogy, so I'm happy to talk with some-body about it for a change."

So far, so good. "What ever happened to Franklin Merton after he left Majestic? Did he return to the family home?" I didn't know where the family home was, but this family genealogy keeper could fill in the blanks to the mystery of Helene and Franklin.

"He never returned. Nobody ever heard from him again. He just dropped off the face of the earth." He was matter of fact.

"The local paper claimed he was either chased out of town or paid off by the husband of the woman he had an affair with." I shared, hoping he could give me anything.

"Nope. Franklin's sister used to get two or three let-ters every month from Franklin, but suddenly they just stopped. I have the letters, saved them from being tossed when my parents were clearing out an attic. In the letters, he confided to his sister all about his love for Helene, but her husband refused a divorce and tormented her. Franklin seemed depressed about the entire mess and yet he wouldn't leave. I can't believe he left without Helene and didn't stay in contact with his sister. The family has always believed he died suddenly and nobody knew who to notify."

"Did somebody in your family try to find out what happened?"

"Oh, sure. The sister's husband traveled to Majestic and asked at the Amherst mansion about Franklin. Mr. Amherst claimed he did not know where Franklin was and to never come around again. So he went to the police for information, and was run out of town."

"You're kidding."

"Honest to God's truth. His diary told about how a policeman threatened him and escorted him a mile out of town. I have the diary, too"

That made me think old Jedediah had the police in his pocket, perhaps with bribes. No wonder nothing ever came of the investigation into Helen's murder.

"That's terrible."

"Yes, but it's interesting." This guy was quite the family historian, saving all the documentation of his ancestors.

"Has anybody ever come around asking about Franklin?"

"Yes. At least, I think so. My father said a young man came to the house and asked about old Franklin and a child of his that had been raised by another family. It sounded strange and my dad's memory was terrible at that point, so we just thought he was confused. Do you think it's for real?"

I shared what I suspected of Helene and Franklin's love child being raised by her close friend to keep it safe from Jedediah.

"I don't have any absolute proof, but it's a good bet.

If that were the case, and your father's memory was correct about a young man asking about Franklin, you could have a living relation you didn't know about."

Before I hung up, I had to know. "Did your father say anything about the guy he met? Any description?"

He took a few seconds, then shared: "Tall. Oh yeah, and he had the Merton family hair. Meaning he had thick black hair that runs strong throughout our family."

"Thank you for all your help."

"I'm getting back on my genealogy site and seeing if there's any new DNA matches to the family. This is exciting. Imagine finding a long-lost relative!"

"If you find him, please call me with his name. It could be part of our investigation."

He noted my contact information and hung up, excited to begin working on this new family mystery.

I took a moment to play "chase the laser dot" with Winston and wear him out, then I stretched out my kinks from sitting so long before continuing.

I grabbed my laptop and logged on to the sites private detectives use for searching missing persons and I had the last known addresses of the three Amherst employees within a half an hour.

None of them lived at the mansion, which wasn't the norm, but since Victoria seemed to travel routinely, maybe that was more convenient with a small staff. It was a sign of how times had changed. The hired help weren't available into the night any longer, they had their own lives.

I slipped out of my room to find Kathlyn, the maid, and find out what was going on today for the house guests. I found her setting out the breakfast buffet for the twenty couples in the dining hall. Only a handful were up this early and ready for sustenance. I caught her attention and motioned for her to join me in the hall. Once we were far enough away so nobody could eavesdrop, I asked if the guests had any plans.

"I've heard they're taking the boat onto the lake for the day. Chef has been busy putting together enough food to last them all day. As soon as the liquor store delivers the booze, they'll likely be out there toasting Victoria while getting sloshed on her dime."

I couldn't help but comment. "Seems more like they're celebrating than mourning." It's as if they aren't even attempting to hide their jubilation over her death. But I couldn't complain because it gave me a perfect opportunity to search their rooms while they're out on the party boat.

"I can't say about most of them, but I know Ainsley was crying on her hubby's shoulder yesterday about regrets of not being closer to Victoria. I don't like Ms. Amherst's ex-husband much, but I saw him shaking his head while looking at her portrait in the great room. He noticed me and said it was just sinking in that she was really gone."

It wasn't much, but I tucked those vignettes away.

"Did you notice anything else yesterday? Any odd behavior, moody or anger, arguments? Anything."

"All the guests are getting bored and drinking too much. At one point Ainsley flat out said they didn't have to stay, the police knew how to contact all of them. They all said it would make them look guilty and they'd stay for the funeral tomorrow." She moved a little closer as if sharing a confidence. "But I think they want to sponge off the Amhersts as long as they can, no matter how bored they are."

"Are you and the other staff staying on full time?"

"It's up to Ainsley I guess. She hasn't told us anything yet. I know Caleb... I mean Chef, is taking off for the rest of the day. With the party boat sailing, he won't have much to cook."

That means I needed to go search his apartment lickety-split before he went home for the day.

"What about Ainsley? Is she going out on the party boat?" I had warned her about taking risks.

"Yes, she seemed to be playing hostess now." Kathlyn finished.

She told me where I could find Ainsley and I zipped off to find her. I found her in the sun room and immediately wished I was wearing sunglasses. It was filled with plants, but even that didn't counter the effects of the sun beaming down on me. She was in a wicker chair typing on a laptop.

I found a spot of shade to stand in. "Ainsley, I warned you to be careful. Please reconsider going out on the party boat. It's simply too dangerous. I can't protect you out there." I wanted her to realize she was taking unnecessary risks.

"I appreciate your concern, but I've thought about it. I should be safe enough. I'll be surrounded by people at all times out on the water. I think the risk is minimal. Besides, aren't you working on finding Victoria's killer now? You aren't on protective duty, and I'd rather you continue helping the police."

"But, I –"

"You aren't protecting me. Go help the police." She turned to her laptop and started typing again.

I had been dismissed along with my warning. I left the sun room and considered her words. True, I wasn't on protective duty any longer. I couldn't protect somebody who didn't want my help. It didn't stop my concern over the situation.

I peeked into the kitchen. It appeared Chef Caleb was nearing completion of his preparations for the party boat. If I was going to search his place, I had better skedaddle. I zipped out to my car and zoomed away.

I parked a couple of blocks away from Caleb

Naylor's address. I was grateful for the cloudy and dreary day. Not only did it match my mood, but I suspected I would be even more drained without it.

It was a mixed neighborhood, with apartments alongside businesses. I ran through the alley at lightning speed. I slowed to approach Chef Caleb's apartment and was able to just walk inside.

I located his apartment on the third floor, but aside from kicking the door in, which was loud and obvious, I hoped I could find a quieter and less conspicuous way inside. Being seen or caught was to be avoided at all costs. What I was doing wasn't police approved and it would only get my boss, Jared Hunter, in trouble for not keeping me in line during a job.

At least Chef Caleb's apartment faced the alley rather than the street, so there was less chance of being seen getting in through a window. I took my time in the shadows of a tree and studied the building.

It was smooth on the exterior, which didn't provide finger or toe holds for me to climb up to his window. I still understand my new abilities, so I wasn't sure if I could jump and grab the window sill, let alone the window be unlocked and so forth. But I had to try because I wasn't dilly dallying on this investigation any longer.

There was a tree in the back, but I didn't like my chances of leaping from a tree limb. Nope, it was time to try a run and jump, like in the sport of high jumping. I did high jump in high school, so this shouldn't be too difficult. Not that I was very good at it even then, let alone now. I just wouldn't be sailing over the top of a bar, I'd be grabbing the slim window sill.

I backed up several feet, inhaled deeply and charged the wall of the apartment building, planted my feet like a gymnast and jumped directly up... and passed his window. I really needed to test my abilities, so I knew what to expect. On the way back down, I grabbed the windowsill and managed to not hurt my arm from the abrupt stop. Dang, I didn't expect that.

My athletic shoes scrambled for traction and I pulled myself up, anchored an arm, and used the free hand to claw at the window. It was awkward turning my hand upside down to push the bottom of the window frame. The window slid up with only a weak squeal of protest. Once I had clambered inside with the grace of a hippo, I took a moment to thank the universe he left his window unlocked.

Caleb's place was a small one bedroom with traditional taste in decor with lots of green and gray, making it a bit dull for my taste, but masculine. I wasn't surprised it was clean and tidy since I thought of chefs as precise and exacting.

I systematically went through all his desk drawers looking for documents or anything that may give a motive or connection to the Amherst factory or family. I found a journal with information on his family and genealogy search which I snapped a photo with my phone to look at more later. I remembered how Caleb made a point of saying he didn't know Victoria or Ainsley rather than simply say he didn't know anyone in the Amherst family. Perhaps he had some connection in his family history. It was a long shot, but the only possibility thus far.

Tucked inside the journal was an old black-and-white tintype photo of a man in front of some flowering bushes. He had his shirt sleeves rolled up, exposing tanned, muscled arms. There was something that seemed familiar. I continued to stare at the image, hoping my memory would be kind and help me out.

It dawned on me how this man looked similar to the waltzing ghost that night with Helene. Not the same, but there was a definite likeness… and a head of thick, dark hair. What had Franklin Merton's living relative, who was the family historian, said? His father said the man who came asking about Franklin had the Merton hair: thick and black.

Could it be, could Caleb be the living proof of Franklin and Helene having an illegitimate child that grew up out of the reach of a vengeful Jedediah? Even if it meant he was descended from Franklin, it wasn't proof in itself that he killed Victoria. I hadn't found any cigarettes or flash paper. Nothing to even hint he was the letter writer. Nothing on the French revolution among the few books around.

My attention was pulled to the noise of voices in the hallway. My sensitive vampire ears clearly heard the voice of a female resident welcoming Caleb and I let out a whispered *crap!*

"You're home early today! *Lucky you.* How did you manage that?" I could imagine a pretty young woman flirting with Caleb.

I used my phone to snap some photos and shuffled the journal and photos together and put them in the drawer where I found them.

"Just happened that way today. Pardon me, I really need to take a load off since I had to go in early this morning." He was trying to get away from his neighbor, but I hoped she delayed him a little longer.

I had climbed out the window and was dangling from one hand as I lowered the window. It was almost closed when it stuck with only an inch left open.

"Maybe we can get together later and I can help you relax." Her voice was getting low, and there was no mistaking her suggestion. I heard keys in the door lock. I'd run out of time.

I abandoned closing the window and dropped. I thought I would do a nice roll when I hit the ground like you see in the skydiving scenes from movies, but here again I landed on my feet, stumbled and face planted. Nice.

Weren't vampires graceful and ethereal? Apparently

not in my case, naturally. I already felt sore, but I jumped up and ran around the corner to avoid being seen.

Fortunately, I hadn't broken anything, but I was limping a bit from that completely wrong landing and I suspected my vampire status was all that kept me from seriously injuring myself. I still had my phone intact, which was the important thing with its photos of the journal, the only thing I'd gathered from this venture into breaking and entering.

I got to my car and used my rearview to assess the damage from falling on my face. Just some dirt and a few leaves in my hair. I used my sleeve to wipe my face mostly clean. I removed some grass and a golden leaf from my hair and took a moment to gather myself. After several deep breaths, I was ready to continue on and search gardener Ethan Spencer's home.

Ethan lived about a mile away in a block of tri-level townhomes smashed together. The bottom floor was the garage and a two story home stacked on top. They were narrow, with not much to them and no grass or yard. Only a few anemic trees were scattered about, already bare of their leaves.

I surveyed the neighborhood, scrutinized every home with windows, and didn't find a soul watching. I closed my eyes and focused on any heartbeats around me. I detected a few pets at home and one person several doors down who seemed to be sleeping from the relaxed heart rhythm. Apparently most everyone was away, and I thanked my lucky stars or horoscope or whatever.

It took no effort to walk to the back, where I found a cramped little elevated deck I easily vaulted. Within seconds, I found the big picture window left unlocked and climbed inside. Caleb's place was all coordinated and could have had a professional interior decorator pick everything. But Ethan's told a different story.

Nothing matched. The steel blue couch and deep red side chair weren't even close to the same decades or styles. The skinny coffee table was cheap particle board, and the television sat atop a clunky dresser-drawers. My guess was they were all thrift store items.

What surprised me as I zoomed through the compact two floors was the pictures of a family on the staircase walls, Ethan with a woman and two children. But there was no evidence of either living there. Was it a divorce or something more tragic? Those pictures were the only evidence of a past or family of any kind. Nothing else existed to suggest he had much of a life.

I was in his bedroom at a narrow little desk with a laptop (password protected) when I opened a drawer to find a stash of greeting cards. Several from a brother, I surmised, and some friends from high school. Finally, some indications the man wasn't a cover identity and actually had a three-dimensional life.

Mixed in the pile were a few over the years from Priscilla Suthers. Well, this was interesting. She had said she exchanged holiday cards with old Amherst employees, but this seemed more like friends with encouragement. Perhaps they had dated a time or two, who knew. Priscilla even sent a few letters.

I held an envelope and hesitated. All this was a tremendous violation of Ethan's privacy. I certainly knew what that felt like after my own breakin. But, there is the matter of Victoria's murder, and ultimately that won out.

I took a breath and read the letter. It was more like a newsletter with job fairs, including nearby towns and job hunting advice. It appeared that Priscilla may have started her own consulting for the jobless or some such service under the name of Suthers Employment Coaching that the copyright information at the bottom proclaimed. There were a few holiday cards from her as well, but nothing more personal.

I hadn't found anything to suggest he was a prior Amherst employee and in a small town like Majestic, it wasn't unusual for an employment coach to know Ethan, let alone send him newsletters or cards. True to Majestic, paper was still used more than electronic, particularly when you wanted to give a more personal touch. I tucked the contact with Priscilla away. I carefully replaced the window screen when I left so I didn't leave a trace of my visit.

That was all I had for the effort. The former Human Resources manager seemed to have found a new mission trying to assist the many jobless in town in their hunt for gainful employment. Ethan may have had a family at one time but didn't seem to any longer. Odd how he flirted, but still had pictures of his wife. It didn't seem he was over whatever loss happened.

CHAPTER SIXTEEN

I saved Kathlyn's place for last. Sure, the Portland FBI said the killer was probably a male, but I wasn't willing to exclude her as involved. She was in the Amherst house when I ran in so she could have set the fire as a distraction while somebody else whacked Victoria over the head.

Kathlyn was only a few blocks from Ethan's and these were all homes with nice yards. Her address had a two-car garage plus two cars parked on the street. I sat for a while and observed a young woman leave the house in a rush, jog across the lawn, and get into a car parked along the street, and zoom away like she was seriously late. Yep, it was looking like Kathlyn had roommates or perhaps a significant other.

I opened the car window and once again I closed my eyes and focused on my surroundings. I let in the many sounds I usually filter out. Several dogs and cats sleeping in the houses up and down the street, plus a bird of some sort, but not in Kathlyn's place. But I detected a human with a resting heartbeat.

Maybe if I was careful, fingers crossed, I could snoop around and never disturb the sleeping human. This would all be easier if I had the mythical vampire ability to mesmerize, or do the Jedi mind trick. If I were caught in the house, I could mesmerize them and make them forget I was even there, after I used the power like a truth serum to question the person. Yep, it sure would make my job easier.

I let out a deep sigh and got out of my car. I snuck through a few backyards, jumping fences when necessary. I was getting a handle on my jumping but should still test the limits of jumping, strength, and running at some point, so I was better prepared and understood my abilities.

Kathlyn's backyard was a haven for weeds and received little to no attention. I tried the backdoor and hoped the trend of not locking up in this small town would hold, but no, it was secured tight. I found windows to three bedrooms and took my time listening to pinpoint which had a resting human in it. The middle one. Fortunately, this was a one-level with a basement, so I didn't have to do any jumping this time. I started with the room to the left of the occupied bedroom, but it was actually locked. The other was as well. Naturally, the occupied room's window was unlocked. I looked up at the sky and whispered. "Really? This isn't funny, universe."

I hopped up and balanced on the windowsill on my stomach until my eyes adjusted to the interior. For a few moments, I felt like I was in the Olympics for gymnastics balancing on a thin slab of wood. The bed was next to the window and had a young man, resembling a wrestler on television, laying on top of the covers and wearing only his boxers, of course. I was not amused. I wiggled forward until I could get a leg up and over, but I tipped face forward. I caught myself before bashing into the floor, butt in the air, with one foot still on the windowsill. I lowered myself to the floor and got my feet together before trying to crawl to the door so I could search.

A mumbled growl came from the man. "The edge...

too close." His hands twitched and his breathing was ragged. "Falling, can't stop." It was a stage whisper and probably couldn't be heard outside the room. His breathing was more gasps of air.

Without a thought, I whispered back. "It's only a dream. It's your dream. You can do what you want." Not that I had ever changed a nightmare, but it was worth a try. His hands twitched less, but his eyes were still rapidly moving under the eyelids. "Take a deep breath and use your wings." I added. Then I slipped out of his room and into the living room. I would search this last if I had time. I didn't think the evidence I was looking for would be left where roommates could find it or ask questions about it.

I searched the bedroom to the right, but the closet told me this wasn't Kathlyn's since there weren't spare Amherst uniforms. In the other bedroom to the left of the sleeping giant, I found two spare uniforms. I went through all her clothes, her books and desk, and items on the closet top shelf. She didn't have any cards or sentimental items. The only paper was a few bills mailed to her, and those didn't tell me anything. Her bedside table drawer had some nicotine patches. That was interesting since the staff all denied smoking. But, she could be several days or even weeks into quitting and consider that not smoking.

I sat on the end of the bed and looked around. My eyes stopped on the trash can with a few items. My last thing to search. It contained a crumpled computer printout, stained with some cola. The printout was of the award ceremony I had found of the award used to hit Victoria over the head. It was the same picture I had found online and she could have been curious, just like I was. As tempting as it was to look at the nicotine patches and the printout as some sort of proof, I couldn't jump to that conclusion. I needed something more concrete than easy to explain coincidental items.

I looked over the shared living room and found nothing further. Rather than risk waking up the only male in the house, I opted to leave via the back door. I again replaced the window screen and slipped away, hopefully leaving no trace of my visit.

On the drive back, I turned over in my head the suspects. As much as I thought the guests Ashton and Brooklyn could have motives, it made more sense for me to look at the ex-husband, Finley, and his son, Graham, since they both knew the mansion and grounds well enough to set the fire and kill Victoria for the inheritance. Even if they hadn't inherited everything, they likely assumed that Victoria would leave everything to somebody more business savvy.

I stopped at the only all-purpose store in town and walked directly to the baby aisle. I was going to bug the guests without Rowen's magical aid, and a baby monitor was my best mundane option. I considered the options and decided audio only would probably handle it best. The video options would likely be too obvious and discovered quickly. I got two transmitter units to one receiver and paid a bit more than I wanted to get extended range for the mansion. I stocked up on spare batteries too but, if I had my way, this would all be wrapped up fairly quickly.

The Amherst grounds still seemed in mourning, with monochromatic sky and landscaping in gray with crows dotting the trees and grounds. It was more than the lackluster sunshine. It was very apparent to me since I usually saw more vibrant colors as a vampire, but not in the last few days on the lakeside property. It wasn't natural. Mundane humans would've noticed, but nobody had, so I could only believe that it was me. As a vampire, was I aware of murderous currents that manifest in nature around me? Or perhaps Victoria's blood being spilled on the property affected the house and grounds like a sort of mourning. Whatever it was, it reminded me I needed to solve this murder and bring justice before the killer left.

I continued to use the bedroom window to come and go, just to have an edge over the suspects so they didn't easily know where I was. I unpackaged the baby monitors and installed the batteries. Now to hide them in the game room and music room. I hoped they would still be out on the boat so I could plant them quickly.

I popped my head out the door, closed my eyes, and let my senses reach out. I could hear one person moving around in the other wing, probably Kathlyn. Her heartbeat was steady. I sprinted through the halls and down stairs. I placed a monitor in the game room where Rowen had hidden the enchanted cell phone in a planter. In the music room, I didn't want it too close to the stereo or the piano. I tucked it in a decorative bowl of dried flowers on a coffee table in a furniture grouping meant to encourage conversation.

I paused before rushing out the door. This was the room where Rowen and I waltzed. That was such a magical night, let alone the fact that we shared the room with two dancing ghosts. The late Helene Amherst and her gardener lover. I was never a girl who read romance novels or dreamt of a perfect wedding. I'd never known parental love, so I had no reason to expect love would come into my life. So, I say affirmations to attract romantic love, but mostly to believe in it. But dancing with Helene and her gardener made me a believer. They saw only one another when they were in each other's arms. The pure love that shone in their eyes was palpable and alive. Then, to be in Rowen's arms was more than I ever expected already.

If Helene and her gardener could even find each other after death, I would hold on to Rowen and I, finding a way to make our relationship work in the here and now. I stood with my back to the door and whispered, "Helene, I wish you and your love happiness." A gentle breeze laced with perfume stirred my hair and she whispered back, *"please find where he's hidden away."* I wasn't sure what that really meant, but didn't expect to have an actual conversation, so I turned and left.

But the words stayed with me as I walked down the hall. *Find where he's hidden away.* She had to be referring to her lover, the gardener, Franklin. But what did she mean that he's hidden away? It was never proven, but widely suspected Jedediah Amherst killed his wife, Helene. But what if he killed Franklin Merton as well and got away with it? Back then, he could have claimed to fire the man and say he left town with nobody the wiser. There was something at the edge of my mind nagging me about Franklin, but I couldn't bring it into focus. I wanted to solve the puzzle of Franklin Merton being hidden away, but I had the recent murder to solve.

I tucked that whispered request aside and checked for heartbeats again. Still only one in the house. I sprinted to the family wing thinking that Finley and Graham had lived here before, so they would stay in the family section rather than with guests. If Victoria invited them, that seemed reasonable. Perhaps Finley and Graham even expected to stay in the family wing. When Graham's bed was set on fire as a diversion, I think it was in the family wing. I mentally thanked Kathlyn for the initial tour of the house on my first day here. I found the family rooms easily enough, and the fire damaged one still had tape at the door. I began opening doors until I found a room being occupied.

I found Graham's room he moved to after the fire. I recognized his suitcases that I had saved from the fire sitting in a corner. There was no evidence of smoke residue on them. Kathlyn must have scrubbed them clean. I couldn't imagine Graham or his girlfriend doing it.

This should be easier than the staff homes earlier, since it was just the bedroom and adjoining bath. Graham had unpacked, so the suitcases were empty. I zipped through drawers of clothes and various other things, as well as the compact desk with drawers. He left his laptop on the desk, but nothing in the drawers. I was amazed that he left the laptop on, but in sleep mode. It asked for a password. I had read that millions of people use one of ten incredibly simple and common passwords, so I started with the ones I remembered. Sadly, Graham had gone with the pathetic "password" default for his laptop, and I was logged in after only seconds.

I went to his email program that was in his browser and found his online email program. I clicked on it and abracadabra, I was in his personal email. I could read and click through emails sent and received faster than the computer could respond. I stopped cold when I found an email he sent to a private email that gave no hint as to the owner, but it was addressed to Lex, which could be male or female. Alex, Lexi, Alexander or Alexandra, etc and so on. But it was the content of the email, written the next day after Victoria was murdered, but before the will was revealed.

I hope to repay you in full in the next few months. I should have the money by then and once that is done, I don't want to see you ever again.

Short and to the point. Lex could be a loan shark, or a friend who lent him a significant amount of money, and they are no longer friends. Those were the only scenarios that came to my mind. Whatever the situation was, he thought he would have money in a few months. I don't know if he was thinking Victoria's will would somehow leave him money and he would see it that quickly. I always heard stories of how long large estates took to settle the money end of wills. There could be another source of money, too. This proved nothing more than Graham owed somebody money and hoped to resolve it in a few months. He could be selling something for the money.

I took a photo of the screen with my cell phone and put the laptop back to sleep. I finished my search at high speed and found nothing further. At the door, I paused and focused on heartbeats, one still in another wing.

I exited Graham's room and found the one across the hall was also in use. I ducked inside. This one had expensive luggage with leather trim and a vintage look tucked in a corner, so it had to be Finley's room. I repeated the high-speed search while still being discreet and careful. I found nothing, bupkis. The luggage was the last item. I opened one after the other and sifted through everything, careful to leave items as I found them. I stopped when I came to Finley's golf gloves. Could they be the same gloves as were in the video? They were black in some sort of material I wasn't familiar with, not exactly neoprene but similar.

I pulled up a screen shot of that short video that was posted on the web holding the murder weapon. Could this be the same glove? It wasn't the best still shot from the video, but it didn't seem like a run-of-the mill glove. The one in the video seemed to have a tear below the thumb section, and Finley's golf glove didn't. So close, but not a match.

A noise shot through my ear. I focused and could hear an argument approaching. I glanced out the window overlooking the lake and saw the party boat had just made it to the private dock and was being tied down.

A loud slurred voice exclaimed. "You keep your eyes and hands off my wife."

Oh great, they'd been drinking most of the day, and after being thrown together under stressful circumstances, they inevitably were taking it out on each other. This could get ugly. I replaced the gloves and put everything back as I found them in seconds and was out the door, zipped down the hall and made my way to my room and the baby monitor receivers. Winston was asleep on the bed, and I smiled in relief. I hadn't gotten to Ainsley's room and I may not get to before they leave. Although, if I was being honest, I didn't think she had done it. But I should have searched her things as well.

Winston looked up through slitted eyes, as if I was rude to disturb him, and laid his head back down.

It took the guests a few minutes to make it into the house and gather. I focused on heartbeats and found two had gone to their rooms and were in no hurry to join the others, apparently. I hadn't quite learned to tell what emotions raced through a person from their heartbeat. I don't know if that's even possible, but it was more attainable than compulsion. I'd have to work on it, see if I might be a lie detector or something.

As I sat waiting for anything useful in their interactions, I went over everything in my head. Two of the staff thought Finley was the killer, and they likely had seen them interact, so they might have good instincts on that. But two family members pointed to Brooklyn, and they would likely be in a position to know as well. Odds were certainly in favor of the ex-husband, but if the prenuptial agreement or divorce specified he wouldn't inherit anything from Victoria, he wouldn't have any motive. Unless he felt he could hire a lawyer and force the issue because of Ainsley not having any interest nor knowledge of the business.

The outliers in the polling were Ainsley per gardener, Ethan and a Majestic resident per Brooklyn. I'd have thought Brooklyn would have pointed a finger at the obvious and easy Finley. But she wasn't around much and her tale about the angry picketers seemed to have made quite an impression on her. It was also surprising for Ethan to be the only one pointing to Ainsley claiming a sibling wanting to inherit. Nobody, not even Finley or Graham, who were potentially wanting to inherit, pointed to Ainsley.

Did Graham know his dad was unlikely to inherit, or did Graham count on some inheritance to get out of debt? Of course, I couldn't overlook Ainsley killing her sister to inherit everything. She could've planned to sell the company and kill for the piles of cash. She didn't have to run the company to benefit from it financially. But motive was only part of it. Everyone but Graham had access to Victoria. Graham was running right behind me because of the fire and was beside me when her body was discovered. Unless he had an accomplice, like his father. Finley and Ainsley had access.

There was also the capability to do the deed, to kill up close and personal. That award looked heavy, and Victoria was above average height for a woman and it takes a lot of power to swing it and hit hard enough for damage to the skull. Could Ainsley physically do it-in one blow? It seemed like Victoria was struck down with one blow and by surprise. Otherwise Victoria may have called out or defended herself and the killer would've been seen. But the killer moved fast, providing a few seconds for the video with nobody noticing.

Then there was the staff. I hadn't found a definite motive for any of them unless they were connected in some way to the warehouse closure. I had gone through all the files for any employee laid off by the closure and found none of the staff's names. But the chances of a strange person from town being on the grounds, making his way into the house to set a delayed fire, and kill, seemed fantastic.

The second baby monitor came to life, the one I had placed in the music room. Ainsley's voice spoke softly.

"I'm telling you, Will. I know there was a bullet that

just missed me. You saw the hole in my sleeve. I felt the jerk on my sleeve and a *zing* sound."

"Don't be so melodramatic. That hole could've been from snagging your sleeve on a nail or something. I didn't hear any gunshot."

"Haven't you ever heard of a silencer, Will? You know that gal private-eye said I could be a target, but I guess you won't believe it until I've been shot. I know what happened. So nice to see your concern for my safety." Ainsley and her husband didn't seem to be doing well. But to disregard a shot at her was cold-hearted.

I heard the door open and after a few seconds I heard Ainsley mutter, "If you hadn't been standing next to me, I'd suspect you." She let out a few swear words towards her husband and then footsteps going away.

CHAPTER SEVENTEEN

he killer attempted to shoot Ainsley while on the lake. Most of the suspects were on the boat with her. The silencer would have helped if the group was as noisy as I expected they were. I had glimpsed the boat in my initial checking of the grounds before the party. It was quite an impressive catamaran and a guest could have hidden the gun in a big tote bag and simply shot through it, so it stayed out of sight.

With the noise of their drunken revelry, chances were good nobody would even notice. If the gun were fired while in a bag or similar, it would also explain why the killer missed without proper aim. But the shooter could've been among the trees on either side of the house as well. This attempt didn't eliminate suspects at this point. But it confirmed the target was Amherst heirs.

I heard a noise and looked up to see a crow sitting on my windowsill, pecking at the windowpane. I tilted my head and he, or she, tilted his. He danced a little, like he was excited. I stood up, and he flew into the trees.

I stood at the window while I listened to a few of the guests gather in a room where I left a baby monitor. They were setting up the remaining food. Some left to get soda or tea from the kitchen. It sounded like many were switching to non-alcoholic libations for the evening.

I watched the crow flit from one tree to another. I couldn't let down Mr. Hunter further. I already took this case and failed to protect Victoria. I had to catch the killer. My shoulders sagged, and I rested my forehead against the cool windowpane. It was my inexperience and lack of training. I guess the police weren't fairing much better, not that it was any comfort. It was only a matter of hours before the guests left. The employees might not stay and their leaving wouldn't raise suspicions after a murder here.

The little tidbits I'd found today weren't enough to truly incriminate any one person. None of the employees lived here, so they didn't have rooms here to search. My head snapped up. Except for the kitchen, where Chef Caleb practically lived. The police had already searched the kitchen within the first few hours, but we knew little at the point, like the killer used flash paper and a cigarette. It couldn't hurt to do my own search, just to be thorough.

I waited several minutes until heartbeats sounded like they were away from the general areas of the kitchen. I sped along while keeping my steps light so as not to create sound on the floor below mine just in case they reverberated in the old house.

I breezed into the spacious kitchen with the European flare. It seemed bigger without Chef Caleb chopping vegetables and bustling around. If he was a descendant of Helene and Franklin's child, as I suspected, he might be exacting revenge. I began searching cabinets, drawers, the spice rack, and the two refrigerators. Where was the pantry? There had to be more than what I found. I gently tapped and found a decorative panel was actually the door to an expansive walk-in pantry.

I moved every single item and shook many. Nothing. I had to find something or the killer would likely get away with Victoria's murder and Ainsley could be next.

I stopped at the round table where Rowen had sat and ate just a couple days ago and stared out the window. I sighed. Where else should I be looking? The only people left were the guests, particularly Austin and Brooklyn. But they didn't live here, neither arrived early, according to Detective Shields, so they probably weren't familiar with the grounds. The menacing letters were delivered from somebody in town.

The crow flew to the window where I stood, staring. He pecked at the glass like he was getting my attention. I bent down to look at him. He cocked his head, then turned and flew in the same direction as before.

What was in that direction? I realized one place I had completely forgotten and slapped my forehead. I had no clue if the police had searched it, but that would have been the first day when they were still looking for what the murder weapon even was. I don't think they had ever returned and searched any further.

I ran to the sitting room and out the patio doors. I ran across the flagstone patio and off into the trees. That first day, when I was preparing for the party and familiarizing myself with the grounds, I had met Ethan at a gardening shed. I needed to search that shed to be sure.

Within seconds I screeched to a halt in front of the shed door with a sturdy padlock securing it. The crow sat in the tree above and eyed me. The shed was spacious but no convenient window left open or unsecured. I glanced around. There was nothing I could use to remove the lock. I eyed the shed. It appeared to be solid, even the glass enclosed part for seedlings.

I tested the door, and it didn't give. I tested the walls and glass enclosed area. It all seemed well built and secure. If I tried to rip the door off, how much noise would I make? Or broke through a glass section? If it was loud enough, would somebody in the house call the police? The last thing I needed was a charge of breaking and entering, and then there end up being no evidence inside.

I had to search it. It was the last place I could think of to look. I grabbed the padlock and realized I didn't need to rip out the door, just tear off the latch mechanism with the lock, then the door was free. Surely the latch wouldn't make that much noise. I had no clue if I was strong enough, but I kept saying I needed to test my new abilities. I learned I could really jump high today without even giving it my all.

I got a strong grip on the padlock with one hand and braced the door from moving with the other. I took a breath and yanked. There was a slight ripping of the screws, but I was holding the padlock with the latch free.

I ducked inside and moved around in the dark with ease. It was all the way against the back wall, in a corner. The gloves from the video. I held them up by the wrist edge with my two fingertips and studied them. There was the little tear I saw below the thumb in the video. This had to be the gloves. Of course, the police tech would have to test them. I prayed there was evidence left on them.

I dropped them back where I found them and looked around more. Between a worktable and a steel cabinet, I saw something white and cylindrical wedged on the floor. On my knees, I grabbed the work bench's leg and moved it just a few millimeters to snag the item and pull it out. A never lit Morley cigarette, probably rolled away and dropped between the worktable and cabinet unnoticed before the rest of the pack was destroyed. I left it partially sticking out for the police.

I whipped my head around. I had been so focused

on my discoveries I hadn't paid attention to all the myriads of sounds always crashing in around me with my hearing. I had gotten too used to tuning it out unless I focused for a heartbeat. Now there was a heartbeat approaching and heavy footsteps.

Within seconds I was outside, gently closing the door. There was nothing I could do about the latch and padlock now. Anybody could see they were forcibly removed. I put some distance between myself and the shed in the opposite direction of the approaching person. From the heavy clomping steps, I was betting on a man. Could Finley or Graham have used the shed? Given special access since they used to live here? I doubted that was likely.

I was behind a full evergreen for cover with its massive tree trunk and branches nearly to the ground. I saw Ethan approaching in the distance. I took my cell phone from my back pocket. I turned off the sound and texted Detective Shield's cell phone he had called me from earlier. He probably didn't want me to have his personal number, but I saved it when the caller-id said it wasn't the police department. I sent "SOS Ethan, at gardener's shed." It would still take them several minutes.

I immediately ran through what I knew about him. He was hired about six months ago, but how long had he been unemployed? He had pictures of family at his place, but no evidence of them in his life and job hunting notices. If he had been part of the Amherst layoffs, he may have struggled with regular employment.

I knew far too many families went bankrupt and even got divorced over the Amherst closure that had long-term impacts. I remembered he seemed jaded about wealthy families when he pointed the finger at Ainsley. The flirting could have been to throw me off track or be compensation for his broken family.

Ethan stopped at the shed. "What the he…" I heard

him turning in a circle, no doubt checking if he was being watched. Then he threw the door open and charged inside.

I wanted to run to the house and just wait for the police, but even as fast as I could run I'd be crashing through the autumn leaves all around. Since the lawn party when Ethan had last gathered fallen leaves, there were enough birch, ash, and maple trees among the evergreens on the property that my passing would make a racket with the recently dropped leaves.

I couldn't guarantee Ethan couldn't enter the house with his knowledge of the place and perhaps use one of the guests to stop me.

What was I afraid of anyway? He didn't know I was a vampire, and I wasn't easy to hurt or kill. I just needed to keep him from escaping here so he couldn't get to town and flee, disappearing with the gloves. He probably didn't know about the cigarette and I couldn't count on there being any prints on that. No, the gloves were critical.

He came out of the shed and stalked around it. I peeked through the branches. He was scanning the area with the gloves sticking out of his back pocket. He ran a hand through his hair. He went back into the shed and came out with a shovel and a can. He dug a hole quickly, only a foot or so deep, dropped the gloves in the hole, then grabbed the can... a gasoline can.

I burst out of my hiding place and covered the hundred yards in less than a second. I yanked the can out of his hand and threw it as far as I could, which was a good distance before a tree stopped it.

He whirled around and snarled. The flirtatious and pleasant man was gone, without a trace. His eyes were full of anger, his mouth pressed tight, and jaw clenched.

"What're you doing with the gasoline, Ethan?" I said, as if I didn't know.

"None of your business. You wouldn't happen to know who broke into the shed?"

"I didn't see anybody enter the shed." Which was technically true. I kept the hand with the padlock behind my back.

He walked around me, and I lowered my head but kept my eyes on him as I matched his steps and kept facing him. The predator in me felt he was challenging me, and rather than fear, I felt defiant and exhilarated.

"How're you doing that?" He pointed at me.

"What am I doing?" I snarled.

"How're you making your eyes glow red?" He demanded.

Well, that was new and surprising. Apparently, my eyes glow red when I'm furious. Because I was furious, and yet somehow kept the wild urges to lose some whoop-ass on him in check.

"You just bring out the playfulness in me, I guess." I said as I continued to face him as he attempted to circle me.

"Little lady, you don't know what you're playing at," He sneered.

"You set a time-delayed fire with a cigarette and flash fire paper as a distraction so you could kill Victoria Amherst when everyone was busy with the house fire. So, I'm dealing with a premeditated murderer. How'm I doing so far?" I smiled with my fangs showing, "You are the one who doesn't know what you're dealing with."

Ethan didn't seem phased. In fact, he missed the fangs all together as he glanced around, assessing how alone we were. "You? I don't care what martial arts you think you know, you can't stop me." He jerked a gun from his jacket pocket.

There was no evidence of gun ownership at his place, nor in the landscaping shed, but that metal cabinet was always locked. Quelle surprise!

"What happened to you? This doesn't seem like you. When did you become a cold-hearted killer instead of a loving father and husband?" *Keep him talking until the police arrive. Or I would have to take him down myself.*

Surprise flared in his eyes just before they narrowed. "In all your digging, didn't you find how I was one of the sad little people whose lives Amherst Industries destroyed to make more profit? Apparently, all the employees are just an inconvenience with all the benefits like health care and paychecks they're forced to provide, not vital assets that made her extravagant lifestyle possible."

I thought about the boxes of carelessly packed employee files. Priscilla had to have known Ethan worked at Amherst and she likely helped him get the job as landscape maintenance, too.

She had the boxes waiting for me, with the records all a jumble, so it would take many work-hours to find anything, but she didn't include his files at all, that would have jumped out when I went through them. She didn't count on vampire speed to race through all of them.

Detective Shields needed to have a talk with her as an accessory.

"Priscilla was helping cover your trail of employment at Amherst, it would seem."

He flashed a small smile before continuing his tirade. "Do you know what Victoria has done in the last three months alone with all the money she made from outsourcing to near slave labor in another country?"

He stopped circling me, intent on his ranting. "She sailed on her two-hundred-million dollar super-yacht for two-and-a-half weeks around the Greek isles, but got bored with that. She had her Gulfstream Jet fly over to pick her up and whisk her away to Lake Como in Italy, and drank three-thousand-dollar bottles of champagne every day and night. That's only one month. She also stayed for a couple of weeks in Côte D'Azur, France, then over to the Ritz in London, where she was chauffeured around in Limos. Once she was tired of that, she jetted off to Fiji. I charmed her personal assistant into telling me about her lifestyle. Don't worry, the assistant only lasted one year, which was ten weeks longer than her prior assistant, from what I was told."

As he ranted about her extravagant lifestyle, I focused on any hint of approaching sirens in the distance. Nothing. I had to draw this out more.

"Is that why you tried to throw suspicion onto Ainsley by pointing me in her direction? You hoped the police might make her life difficult as a suspect for a while?"

"She comes from the same cursed money as Victoria. You can't abuse people for money and that money not become an albatross dragging you down."

"I understand Victoria spent money extravagantly and without care. And I'm sorry you were laid off when she outsourced jobs overseas for more profit to fuel that excess rather than putting back into the employees."

"The Amhersts need to die out. Ainsley and the genetic line must die off. If she hadn't turned away when she did on the boat, I would have taken her out then. The mentality that the wealthy are risking a lot to provide jobs is a boldfaced lie. We must expose the lie and the family must die off now."

That answered the question about whether Ainsley was truly shot at on the party boat. For now, I had to keep him talking. "But what happened to you?"

He looked instantly older, like the thought of his life wore him down just contemplating it. "I went bankrupt and lost everything, including the house. But I still had my wife and kids. I finally found work, but it was five hours away, so I stayed in a tiny little efficiency apartment. The job was long hours and a third of the pay, but at least I was providing for my family. I came home on weekends, but the marriage was failing. Last year she divorced me, and within a few months she remarried and moved away with the kids. Since I didn't have the finances nor housing to keep the children myself, I only get to see them on holidays-if I can afford to travel to Seattle where they live now. I took this job to expose Victoria to the world. But nobody cares, somehow people make excuses for the waste of a life she and other really wealthy people are in reality. That's when I realized I had to make an example of her."

"Listen, I get it. It isn't fair that the working class is sacrificed on the altar of insatiable greed for more money and excess. But, it doesn't justify wasting your life in hate and revenge. Did killing her change your life, bring your wife and kids back to you?" I didn't expect to break through the depths of his revenge fantasy. I just wanted to keep him focused on me. Before I knew what was happening, he whipped out a handgun with a long silencer like in the crime dramas I watched, and exactly like what probably shot at Ainsley earlier. Oh, crap.

I certainly didn't expect him to shoot me with no warning, which is why I didn't react and avoid getting a bullet in the chest. Lesson learned, talking to a homicidal person to stall for time can backfire. I was abruptly knocked off my feet by the blast and looking at the dreary gray sky. Being a vampire made getting shot unpleasant, but I'm sure nothing like what a mundane would experience. It was painful, plenty painful, but that made my vampire sense of survival kick into overdrive.

was back on my feet in a second, maybe a millisecond slower, and facing him with a rage boiling inside me. I'm a peace-loving person, but now I had a powerful desire to yank him off his feet, shake him senseless, and then do some actual harm with my fangs. But the regular "violence gets you nowhere" side of me kept the rabid vampire side in check, for now... by a thread.

I bet my eyes were really glowing red now, for his eyes were huge and he gulped. Guess he finally realized what a predator in his midst felt like. He broke out into a sweat and took a step backward.

"Don't even think about running. You try to act like a frightened little bunny and I can't be held responsible for how I will hunt you down. You see, you aren't the deadliest thing on this property."

My senses were tingling like a live electrical current and I knew every move of every living creature on the property without having to focus. It was a rush and quite intoxicating. "In fact, there isn't a wild beast nor human anywhere close I wouldn't rip apart if they tried to run at this moment." My voice was death itself.

Finally, I heard a siren in the distance, out on the lake road. It would still be a couple of minutes before they arrived. I just had to maintain control and calm down. I couldn't tell Detective Shields how Ethan, the man who tenderly cared for the plant life, was the killer if my eyes were still red with rage.

"Ethan, listen carefully. You have a choice now. You can stay right there and don't move until the police come to arrest you. Or you can try to escape and I'll have to hunt you down. I will play with you and let you think you're actually going to get away, before I drop out of the sky and stop you in a very permanent sense-perhaps painfully, too. Your choice." I put my fangs on full display in a grim smile.

His eyes darted around like a pinball, then settled on me. A calm settled over him and his eyes hardened into a stare. He made the wrong decision. I put on a burst of speed and before he could blink, I was behind him with my arm around his neck. I had to stand on tiptoe to manage it and bend him backward.

It took him a second to realize what had happened.

I whispered in his ear, "You just can't get it through your head. You can't win. You're going to jail. The only other alternative is I deliver justice my way. It's over." Not that I would do anything, I hoped. But he didn't know that.

I held him there, despite of his occasional attempts to break away and his growing fear of *what* had him captive.

I was taking lots of deep breaths to calm my vampire rage. My body was all healed, the pain was gone, and Ethan was on his knees with my arm still around his neck by the time the slow-poke police finally drove up to the house and found their way to us.

"Oh, and I know these cops, and I've worked with them before. You just never know who or what you may be talking to, so behave." I snarled, trying for a threatening note in my voice rather than girlish. It came out as a low snarl.

Detective Shields surveyed my grip on Ethan before motioning for a cop to handcuff him. The gloves he attempted to set on fire were taken into evidence, as well as the cigarette I directed them to. I gave my statement of his confession to me and his working at the factory. I shared how Priscilla obscured, maybe even covered up, the fact Ethan worked at Amherst Industries. Detective Shields assured me Priscilla would facr charges, too.

Ethan studied how Detective Shields and I knew each other. I imagine he was debating saying I wasn't human, but from his staring at the detective, he suspected Shields of not being human either, or at least wouldn't believe any wild claims he made about me.

He refrained from blurting anything. As he was being perp walked past me in handcuffs, I winked at him. I couldn't resist.

I went into the Amherst mansion and found everyone gathered in the music room. The mood was quiet and reserved compared to the raucous group that had returned from the lake.

Ainsley jumped up, "Kathlyn informed me several police cars arrived. What's going on? Did you call them?"

"The police have just made an arrest in your sister's murder. I'll let Detective Shields fill you in on the details, but I caught the killer trying to destroy evidence, and he assaulted me as well."

There was a chorus of gasps with a few exclamations of "Oh," "We can go home," and "It's about time."

I continued, "Ainsley, could I have a few moments with you, please?"

We went to the library and closed the door. We sat in the leather chairs and I jumped in with my thoughts.

"There are two things I need to go over with you. But first, can you tell me what you know about the gardener after Jedediah killed Helene? What happened to him?"

Her brows furrowed. "All I ever heard was that Jedediah *'sent the scoundrel packing.'* Why do you ask?"

"I found a newspaper clipping in the attic that said there was conjecture he'd been paid off to leave town. I believe he was also killed, but the body was never found, so nobody suspected he was dead. I think your ancestor, Jedediah, got away with his murder." I took a deep breath before continuing with the next part. "I suspect your attic may actually have his body."

She gasped. "I always hated that attic. I thought there was a ghost there and Victoria called me a baby for being afraid to go up there. You really think, after all this time, a body is still up there?"

"I recommend getting some imaging equipment brought in to check behind the walls. I suspect once you find Franklin Merton's remains and properly bury them, the attic will be much calmer." I also felt he should be buried near Helene, but I could bring that up later.

"You said two things to talk about. Was there something else?"

I had worked out that Franklin had to be the hostile presence in the attic, but it took reflecting on Helene and her ghostly dancing partner in the game room the other night for me to make the connection to the old tin type photo I found at Caleb Naylor's apartment.

Then I remembered how Caleb was careful to say he had never specifically met Victoria or Ainsley before working here in answer to any connection to the family. His answer had struck me as off at the time but made sense if he was hiding his connection via an ancestor.

It fit with my calls to Helene's family and the story of a tall man with black hair asking about Helene.

"I believe your chef, Caleb, may be related in some way to Franklin Merton... and Helene. The same article I found in the attic mentioned Helene had been gone for a few months and it hinted she had to avoid a scandal, meaning having a baby away from town. If he is of some relation, it would be good to include him in Franklin's burial. Just a suggestion."

"That's quite a claim." She was silent for a moment. "If Caleb is indeed related to the prior gardener, what was he doing here? Was he trying to make a claim on our family? You're sure he wasn't involved in Victoria's death?"

"Caleb isn't the one under arrest, is all I can say. I'll tell you I'm personally positive Caleb didn't kill your Victoria." After the confrontation I had with Ethan, I was sure of that.

"But why would he be here and not tell us of this association with our past?" She crossed her arms.

"He could just be here wanting to feel close to a long-lost family member he'd only heard about. You can understand how complicated family can be, and how sensitive personal family issues are. He may not have shared it because it really had nothing at all to do with you."

"Even so, why should I give any honor to the man who tore Jedediah and Helene's marriage apart?"

"Have you seen Helene's ghost?" She nodded her head slightly, as if reluctant to admit any sightings. "Well, I have. I've seen a radiant Helene dancing in Franklin's arms, not her husband's. Honestly, the man killed Helene, and probably Franklin, too. Over a hundred years later, we can try to judge Helene and Franklin, but those were different times when fathers arranged marriages without a thought to the woman. We don't know what that marriage was like. In fact, I found she asked for a divorce and Jedediah refused and she was stuck. But I know that in the afterlife, Helene and Franklin are the ones dancing together, not Jedediah and Helene."

I finally felt my job was done. I packed up my stuff,

Winston, plus the files, and Kathlyn helped me cart everything to my car.

As I drove down the long drive and looked back in the rearview mirror, I hoped happier days would come to Amherst. The skies still seemed sullen, but I swear the fountain sounded less like tears dripping and more like water splashing, and the trees waved to me as I drove past. I don't know if I ever wanted to return to this property, but I would never forget the last several days.

Now I could return to my life and deal with the increasingly complicated quagmire. How was I going to track down a deadly and pissed off rogue vampire? Then there is the entire situation with Rowen and our struggling relationship.

That is one thing Amherst provided me with, the memory of Rowen and my one dance that I would cherish. It seemed Rowen and I were over before we had a chance to develop into anything. What future was there for us if we had to hide even a dance together? Now I was pretending to date some Casanova vampire in the hope Rowen and I can sneak around to have a simple date.

On the positive side, I couldn't say I was bored.

I stopped at the store and bought a rotisserie chicken Winston would feast on for a week. I owed my sweet feline best friend for everything he had been through. I also got some special pastries for Mrs. Macksimowitz for looking after Winston while I was away.

I parked on the street and settled all my things back in my little sunken basement apartment and moved the boxes of Amherst files to my car. I was in my compact kitchen removing chicken from bone for Winston, who was rubbing up against my legs, when I tuned into Mrs. M upstairs. Mrs. M had a visitor, a male visitor from the deeper voice.

Then I felt him. My stomach plummeted and fear shot through me like a whiskey shot. The rogue vampire was upstairs with Mrs. M. What game was he playing? Mrs. M had nothing to do with him or the Meta world. She was a kind soul. I was upstairs at her door in seconds, ringing her doorbell that sounded like chimes. My mind raced over what I might find the rogue had done.

Mrs. M opened the door, a big smile on her face that disconcerted me.

"Oh Misty, I'm so glad you're home, dear. A friend of yours is here. He was asking me about you. He's been by the last few days and was asking me where you had gotten off to. I told him you had texted me and would be home shortly and he should just join me until you got home."

She led me into her formal living room, a Victorian dream in dusty rose, heavy on the ornate decorative wood scrollwork. On the loveseat sat a man with a rather ordinary face, seemingly in his thirties. His very presence was commanding. He wore denim jeans and a tee-shirt which made him seem normal and non-threatening. Mrs. M seemed her usual kind self, concerned with making him feel at home and completely oblivious to the uber-predator sitting in her house. Couldn't she sense the danger? Didn't she feel anxious, as if a bloodthirsty animal were ready to strike?

I certainly felt it. I was struggling to keep my fangs receded.

"Can I get you something to drink, dear? I have some of that tea you love." She waited for my reply.

"That would be lovely Mrs. M." I said, more to get her out of the room than anything.

She bustled into the kitchen and my smile dropped as I faced an apex predator and monster who turned my life topsy-turvy.

"Don't you dare hurt her. She has nothing to do

with this." My whisper was desperate, but laced with anger.

He tilted his head. "You may call me sire, since I am your sire." His voice lacked warmth and could've been a machine talking.

I raised an eyebrow and placed my hands on my hips as my response.

"I can see respect and manners are still lacking in these modern times."

"You have to earn respect, buster." I ground out. "If you think your complete disregard for my wishes and life just because you can will get you one speck of regard, try again."

He stood and took two steps towards me. "You interest me, Misty. You fight against our nature to be night creatures and insist on existing in *their* world. You keep and care for a pet while maintaining relationships with mundanes and even other Metas." He tilted his head like I was a curious specimen. "And then there's your ability to summon the sun mentally, which no vampire, to my knowledge, has had before."

I *interested him*! Oh, crapola. I didn't want this monster even knowing I was on the same planet.

"Look, Jack, you attacked me and ruined my life. To be honest, I hate everything about you and your entitled mentality that 'might makes right' or 'force equals superiority.'"

He leaned closer to me. "I am the oldest vampire alive, to my knowledge. I've been in royal courts in France and Italy and studied art from the masters, politics with reformers, and astronomy from Galileo. I gave you a gift of superiority to these mundane vermin that have spread the globe and over other Metas. I can help you reach your potential."

What was he really after? He had no interest in me when he took my blood and then turned me. Leif and the council said the others that were turned had no other contact with Jack, yet here he was giving me his *special* attention. I didn't believe it was really about me. He had an ulterior motive.

It had to be the Obtestor Solem where I could conjure the sun mentally, and it affected vampires. When Rowen and I started searching for this rogue, he came at us, and I instinctively used it and stopped his attack. If, as he claimed, no other vampire has ever had that ability, then I was not only rare, but a weapon against other vampires.

That's what he was after, to use me as a weapon to keep not just this Meta council but all of them from interfering in his complete disregard of their laws to live harmoniously alongside other Metas and the mundane world. I had forgotten all about it, but he clearly had been thinking about it.

I really try not to actually hate anybody, perhaps strongly dislike, but not hate. Jack won the prize. I officially hated this creature.

I imagine my Obtestor Solem ability was behind Leif's fear of my getting attached to Rowen, a witch, because I had this power and they didn't have me under their vampire thumb. But I didn't see Leif as the same level of threat as Jack. I wasn't as sure about the entire Meta-Mundane council, though.

"I'll be sure to consult with the Meta-Mundane Council on your offer. From here on out, this entire house is off limits and leave Mrs. M and my cat out of this."

"Oh, did you ask the Council permission to hang with that witch you like? Listen, I don't care who you're interested in romantically, so long as we can work together."

With that, he walked out the door. Mrs. M walked in with my tea and looked around.

"He had somewhere to be and left." I said, leaving an encyclopedia of commentary unspoken.

"Dear, I don't like to get involved, but I didn't get a good feeling about that man. Watch your step around him, okay?" She held my eyes.

"I'm in complete agreement. In fact, don't let him in again. Don't even answer the door if it's him." I don't know if that would matter with Jack Anderson, rogue vampire. I was, however, reassured that Mrs. M's instincts were still on target.

I stood on the lawn in the chill air. It wasn't over with rogue Jack whether or not I liked it. I had no other option than to bring this new wrinkle to the Meta-Mundane Council. As if my life wasn't complicated enough already.

EPILOGUE

$\mathcal{A}$insley had invited me to be present as the attic wall was torn down. Helene was in the shadows observing, her faint image quivering as if she were anxious. The workmen stopped and moved aside. Beyond the hole in the plaster was a dark hole. The supervisor grabbed an oversized flashlight and looked inside.

"Well, I'll be d– !" He stopped mid explicative. "Police need to be called. You've got a skeleton alright." He shook his head like he didn't believe what his eyes were telling him.

Ainsley had contracted a company out of Portland to use specialized equipment to check the attic walls. They reported something atypical behind that specific section of the wall. I was positive about what they would find. I asked Helene to calm her waltzing partner and let the workmen into the attic without his anger and ghost antics.

I whispered to Helene's spirit in the shadows, "Found him. Now we need to get him out of there."

She nodded and smiled before she mouthed a silent *thank you*.

Ainsley turned to me, "As if the town doesn't hate my family already. When it's reported that old Jedediah murdered the gardener on top of his bride, they'll be screaming at the gates."

"Not if you reach out to any living relatives of Franklin Merton and ask them to be present at the formal burial. You can show the town that the current Amherst family will do their best to honor this man's memory. In fact, I have a family contact for you."

She sighed. "You're still pushing me to bury him next to Helene? I checked at the cemetery and there isn't room. But I can get the last plot in that section." She rubbed her temples.

I glanced at Helene and she nodded with what looked like tears in her eyes.

"I think that'll be fine. What about Caleb?"

She started down the stairs, leaving the workmen to remove the rest of the wall so the forensic officer could have easy access, but told them to take photos as they went for documentation and save for her.

"The DNA test shows we are indeed related, and apparently Helene and Franklin's child was raised by a close friend of hers. I met with Caleb and my lawyers. He claims he doesn't want any of the estate or inheritance. He says he just wants to know about his ancestry."

That was good news, but Ainsley didn't seem pleased.

"I sense there's a *but*."

"I've been thinking. The factory is gone, so this place is more a vacation house than a home. Caleb could turn this into a Bed and Breakfast or something special with his cooking skills. It would be nice to give back to the town in some way. I can never reverse the damage that was done when the factory was closed, but maybe this house can have real purpose and benefit Majestic."

"I think that is a great step towards healing in the community. Might I also make a suggestion?"

She chuckled, "Could I stop you?"

"The contact for the Merton family has become the family's historian, and he has letters from Franklin to his sister. Seems part of the story is contained in those letters detailing Helene wanting a divorce, but Jedediah being spiteful and refusing. Also, there is a diary of Franklin's brother-in-law detailing coming to Majestic and being run out of town."

Ainsley's eyes had gotten larger. "That poor woman. And now we know Franklin was murdered, too. No wonder this house always seemed so unsettled and somehow grieving." She glanced my way as if gauging my reaction.

"I was thinking. Maybe you could embrace transparency and pick a room to tell Helene and Franklin's story. If the Merton contact would allow the letters and diary to be on display, keep any news stories about the discovery of Franklin's remains to display. Maybe some items from the attic are Helene's and could be part of the exhibit. This would give Caleb his family connection as well."

She lowered her voice. "Do you think it might satisfy their spirits?"

I looked at Helene in the shadows. She had her hands clasped to her heart and nodded with a smile on her face.

"Yes, I believe it would please them very much."

"Then I will begin work on a space to tell Helene and Franklin's tragic love story, and I'll be sure it places the blame squarely on Jedediah and his role." She rubbed her hands together. "I'm inspired to do a large painting of Helene and Franklin for the display, too."

* * *

FRANKLIN MERTON WAS BURIED in a peaceful and touching ceremony graveside, shortly after his skeleton was respectfully retrieved from the attic wall. Simple but restorative. Everything was photographed for the new exhibit to tell his story.

I wasn't surprised a week or two later when Caleb called and told me the house had been turned over to him. He had plans to make it an event space for weddings, family reunions, and retreats, but also a community theater space. He planned on getting historic status so he could keep it non-lake themed. Guests wouldn't be scared away because ghost sightings had stopped and the attic was quiet now that Franklin's remains had been found.

But I'll never forget that waltz by candlelight.

At least something positive came from the Amhersts for the town after the factory shut down. If only the vile vampire Jack Anderson would have such a change of heart.

AFTERWORD

Thank you for reading!

Dear Reader,

I hope you enjoyed *Second Time Around: Accidental Vampire PI #2*. I really enjoyed writing the characters and the locations! I hope Misty's adventures entertained you, and you are looking forward to the next book, *Strike Three*.

Finally, *I need to ask you a favor.* If you're so inclined, **I'd love a review** of **Second Time Around**. Whether you loved it or hated it—I'd just enjoy your feedback. Reviews can be tough to come by these days. You, the reader, have the power to make or break a book.

Also, feel free to contact me at mysterysuspense1@gmail.com if you have spotted any typos that have escaped my editor and proofreader's attention. Let me know where you found the typos or errors.

Subscribe to my newsletter for exclusive content and specials: tinyurl.com/2p952mcv

Thank you again for reading *Second Time Around* and spending time with me.

In gratitude,

Avery Daniels

ABOUT THE AUTHOR

Avery Daniels was born and raised in Colorado, graduated from college with a degree in business administration, and has worked in fortune 500 companies and the Department of Defense her entire life. Her most eventful job was apartment management for 352 units. She still resides in Colorado with two brother black cats as her spirited companions. She volunteers for a cat shelter, enjoys scrapbooking and card making, photography, and painting in watercolor and acrylic. She inherited a love for reading from her mother and grandmother and grew up talking about books at the dinner table.

Let's stay in touch.

Sign up for exclusives and news of new releases: http://tinyurl.con/2p952mcv

Website: www.Avery-Daniels.com

Goodreads: http://www.goodreads.com/Avery-Daniels

BookBub: www.bookbub.com/authors/avery-daniels